Startled, Bolan recognized Aguillar near the perimeter

He appeared to be constructing a defensive line to meet the column of advancing soldiers. When the terrorist leader had gathered and positioned every rebel who could walk and hold a weapon, he stood waiting for a confrontation with the enemy.

A moment later, as they came through the trees, Bolan saw the uniforms of the Security Police. Gunfire broke out on both sides of the line, but there was something else, as well—the distant sound of helicopter rotors.

Aguillar had heard it, too. With one last look at his men, the rebel leader turned and ran.

The Executioner saw where his duty lay and struck off in pursuit.

MACK BOLAN ®

The Executioner

DON PENDLETON'S
THE EXECUTIONER®
TOUGH JUSTICE

A GOLD EAGLE BOOK FROM
W⦿RLDWIDE®

TORONTO • NEW YORK • LONDON
AMSTERDAM • PARIS • SYDNEY • HAMBURG
STOCKHOLM • ATHENS • TOKYO • MILAN
MADRID • WARSAW • BUDAPEST • AUCKLAND

First edition May 1998
ISBN 0-373-64233-4

Special thanks and acknowledgment to
Mike Newton for his contribution to this work.

TOUGH JUSTICE

Against naked force the only possible defense is naked force. The aggressor makes the rules for such a war; the defenders have no alternative but matching destruction with more destruction, slaughter with greater slaughter.
—Franklin D. Roosevelt

I communicate with terrorists in the only language they understand: brute force. No hungry predator has ever carried out good-faith negotiations in the history of man. Why waste time bargaining with murderers? It's war to the knife, and the knife to the hilt.
—Mack Bolan

To the fighters of terrorism the world over.
Fight the good fight.

PROLOGUE

The traffic had picked up on Avenida Grau by ten o'clock, as Lima's populace caught its second wind and rolled out to the cafés, restaurants and nightclubs. Supper was the late meal of the day in Latin countries, where the midday break for a siesta provided for a leisurely, more laid-back pace. It took a while for Anglos to adjust, accommodate themselves to Latin rhythms, but the vast majority appreciated the change.

The four men riding with Cesar Macario weren't relaxed. Their minds were focused on specific duties, and one or two of them were nervous. Jumpy. They were new to the killing game.

Macario told himself that this one should be easy. They didn't even have to kill the American. They simply had to take him prisoner, then deliver him to those who would be waiting.

Simple.

The American had been followed for a month or more, observers noting every movement when he left the embassy. They knew about his whore in the flat on Avenida Roosevelt. The target went to see her twice a week, Tuesday and Thursday nights, as regular as clockwork. He was most dependable that way, and Macario knew he should feel grateful for a mark who cooperated in his own abduction.

He had never failed yet in a mission for the cause, and

he didn't plan to start this evening. He had brought four men along, and all of them were armed: the driver with a sawed-off shotgun, while the other three had pistols fitted with sound suppressors. Macario had saved the best piece for himself, an Ingram MAC-11 submachine gun, also suppressed. He didn't plan on using it, but he still felt better with the extra firepower at hand.

Guerrilla warfare was a risky business, all the more so in an urban setting, where there was no jungle for concealment and you never knew who might turn traitor in the next five minutes, helping the authorities to stage a deadly ambush. Every move Macario made for the Shining Path was a risk to his life, but he had long since grown accustomed to the pressure, living on the edge.

He sometimes thought about his father, who grew coffee in the mountains near Chincheros, working all his life for just enough to feed a family of twelve, and often falling short of that. No man of vision, he, but Macario had the fire inside him, recognizing the injustices of a society that kept its native people down with violence and repressive laws. He had enlisted in the liberation movement as a teenager, killed his first soldier four months later, and from that point on there was no turning back.

Not that he ever once regretted his decision. It would cost his life if anyone in the Shining Path once suspected he had changed allegiance, but there was no risk of that. Macario had proved himself a hundred times before.

And he would prove himself again this night.

"How far?" he asked the driver, still not used to Lima after all this time. The crowded streets confused him, made him wish that he was in the mountains once again, where he could feel at home.

"We're almost there," the driver replied.

A right turn onto Avenida Abancay, and they were rolling north. Macario reached underneath his jacket just to reassure himself that he hadn't misplaced the Ingram since he climbed into the car. Whatever happened in the next half hour, he would be able to defend himself. And if he lost his life, well, that was part of fighting in a revolution.

He wasn't afraid of death; Macario had seen it and inflicted it too many times for death to hold much mystery. He *was* afraid of dying poorly, though, and ending in disgrace.

He focused on the elevator, the layout of the luxury apartment house they had been studying for days. The Shining Path had a friend in maintenance who had supplied the floor plans and the apartment number of the American's whore. Their friend had planned to call in sick this night, but that would only have increased suspicion. They would have to beat him up a little, make it realistic, but he understood and didn't mind a certain sacrifice for victory.

They would be riding the service elevator to the seventh floor. The passkey would admit them silently to her apartment, give them the advantage of surprise. If she made any noise at all or tried to interfere with them in any way, Macario would kill her on the spot.

He hoped the woman was smart enough to know that and avoid compelling him to shoot her.

They parked in back of the apartment building, and the driver kept the engine running.

Macario reached underneath his jacket, cocked the Ingram and made sure to switch the safety on. The SMG was temperamental, and he had no wish to shoot himself—or anybody else—by accident.

Whatever killing Macario and his men might do this night, it would be calculated and deliberate.

"Let's go," he told his men, and led the way inside.

IT WAS AMAZING, Garrick Hastings thought, how people change. For sixteen years he had been faithful to his wife, had never even thought about another woman—well, maybe he did; but thinking wasn't *doing it,* and now...

He stopped himself before the thought went any further. Kelly had been gone for five years now. You couldn't cheat on someone who was dead and buried, right? It made no sense.

And yet it felt like cheating, all the same. That wasn't necessarily a bad thing, since it added spice to the relationship, along with the intrigue of trying to avoid detection by his people at the embassy. But there was still the guilt that dogged him every time he left Miranda's flat and rode down in the elevator to his car. It was the flip side of excitement that had never failed to summon thoughts of Kelly afterward, making Hastings feel like one of those pathetic creatures on the stateside talk shows, pouring out the details of their seedy, seamy lives before an audience of millions.

It was never like that with Miranda Muñoz.

He had met her at a party at the British embassy, the gist of the occasion long since lost to mind. Nothing had mattered from the moment Garrick saw her face and made his way across the crowded room to introduce himself. His fluent Spanish had surprised her, but she answered him in English, automatically putting him at ease. She had a talent for it, as he soon discovered.

The relationship took time, though not as long as Hastings had imagined. There was something in the Hispanic blood, perhaps—or maybe she liked sleeping with a man who had some measure of authority, however limited. Hastings didn't deceive himself into believing that Miranda had mistaken him for Robert Redford or Mel Gibson. He had a notion that she honestly enjoyed his company, along with all the gifts, and he preferred to think she wasn't faking when she climaxed, but at his age, with the big five-oh approaching like a runaway express train, he would take what he could get.

And never, ever look a gift horse in the mouth.

The odd part was that Hastings had begun to think he loved Miranda. It was just an inkling so far, nothing definite, but he could recognize the signs. He told himself that it was stupid, childish; he was thinking with the little head instead of with the one upstairs. It made no difference.

He wondered if the others at the embassy were all aware of his arrangement with Miranda, laughing at him when his back was turned. He thought someone would probably have mentioned it by now, but you could never tell for sure. Diplomacy was much like any other office job. You could bet money there was someone, enemy or so-called friend, who would make use of any detrimental information they could lay their hands on.

He listened to the shower running, felt a stirring in his loins and wondered if he ought to join Miranda. They had made love twice already—as incredible as *that* might seem for someone his age—but he never got enough of her. She made him feel like...like...

Hastings's mind was groping for an apt analogy when he saw a strange man standing in the bedroom doorway. His first instinct was to retrieve the tangled sheet and hide his nakedness, the second to find out exactly what was going on.

Both thoughts were driven from his mind as the intruder raised some kind of automatic weapon, bulky with the sound suppressor that made it look like something from an old sci-fi serial. The weapon pointed straight at Hastings, roughly at the level of his chest.

"Who are you?" Hastings was amazed to hear his own voice nearly tremor free.

The stranger moved into the bedroom, two more men close behind him.

"Get dressed," the first man ordered, pointing with his automatic weapon toward the chair where Hastings's clothes were strewed without regard to wrinkles.

That was something, anyway. If they were letting him get dressed, it meant they must be taking him somewhere. And that, in turn, offered at least some hope that he was going to survive. If all they wanted was to kill him, they could easily have done the job by now. Of course, there was an equal chance that they would take him somewhere else, for a more public execution, to display his body as a symbol of achievement, but he would not dwell on that.

Not yet.

He had his shorts on and was reaching for his trousers when the shower suddenly switched off. He stiffened, realizing there was no way he could dress and leave the flat with his kidnappers fast enough to spare Miranda. In another moment, she would be emerging from the bathroom. She would see the men, their guns. What if she screamed or got hysterical? What would prevent these men from harming her?

She stepped into the bathroom doorway, sleek and naked, taking in the strange tableau in front of her, making no attempt to cover herself with the towel in her hand.

"It took you long enough," she told the man with the machine gun.

He was staring at her, obviously startled, uncertain how to reply. It struck Hastings then that Miranda's treachery had been complete. The men who came to seize him were no more aware of her duplicity than he had been.

Something snapped inside him, the straw that broke the camel's back, perhaps. Barefoot, bare chested, with his trousers in his hand, he rushed the leader of the hit team, swinging with a roundhouse right, directly at the gunman's face. Hastings was cursing, shouting in his anger, but he never could remember afterward exactly what he said. He saw the punch aimed at his adversary miss by inches as the gunman took a short step backward, swinging up his weapon.

Any second now, Hastings thought, but the gun didn't go off. Instead, its heavy muzzle slammed into his forehead, staggered him, set bells off in his skull. He felt his balance going, tried to compensate by lunging toward another of the kidnappers. Behind him now, he heard the leader of the snatch team.

"Don't shoot!"

Instead of killing him, the second gunman smiled and clubbed him with the pistol he was carrying. The floor rushed up at Garrick Hastings and collided with his face. He knew there would be pain when he woke up, *if* he woke up, but for the moment there was only darkness, coming up to swallow him.

Oblivion was a relief.

1

Mack Bolan had been marking targets for the past twelve hours, haunting Lima and its suburbs like a restless ghost. From Comas on the north, down to Chorillos on the south and all points in between, he had compiled a hit list of addresses, names, enough targets for a day of two of hunting if the game went on that long.

He hoped it wouldn't, though. Experience had taught him that each day he spent in hostile territory multiplied the chances of disaster. His life was riding on the line, had been since he stepped off the plane at Jorge Chavez International, but there were also other lives at stake.

If Bolan failed this time, he failed them all.

His target was Sendero Luminoso, or the Shining Path. Organized as a rural guerrilla army in 1970, seeking to topple the Peruvian government and supplant it with native Indian rule, the homegrown terrorist movement was still going strong after almost thirty years. The Shining Path had brought its war to urban battlegrounds in 1986, and it had proved equally effective in the concrete jungles of Lima, Iquitos, Pucallpa and other cities, adapting its tactics from one killing field to another. From the beginning of its war, the group had staged more than twelve thousand bombings, raids, ambushes, drive-by shootings, with at least ten thousand deaths acknowledged by the government. That probably meant half again as many killed, in fact, and those figures didn't include the casualties inflicted by a violent and erratic government response.

So brutal was the state's attempt to crush the Shining Path, that various observers from the UN and assorted human-rights groups had complained repeatedly of torture, roving death squads and successive military strikes on unarmed villages, sometimes with massacres resulting. A new controversy had erupted in the summer of 1995, with the announcement of an amnesty for any soldier or policeman charged with murder or similar acts of lawless brutality since the long war began. The Shining Path had promptly threatened to "renew" its struggle—which had never ceased, in any case—and broadened its attacks to target foreign diplomats and tourists from a list of countries that supported the existing government.

All that was fairly standard in the kind of dirty war that had been savaging Peru for nearly three decades. The same thing had been going on in Palestine since 1948, in Spain since 1959, in Northern Ireland since 1969. The Shining Path wasn't quite the new kid on the block in these days when a new group seemed to spring up somewhere every other week, nor were its tactics any great surprise. It was the same old story, but with a twist this time.

The "freedom fighters" had a hostage, now. He was American, a well-known diplomat, a man with friends at home. One of those friends, from high-school days, now made his home at 1600 Pennsylvania Avenue. When *that* friend made a phone call, he inevitably got results.

And sometimes, when solution of a "special" problem called for violation of the standard diplomatic protocol, he got Mack Bolan.

It should have been a simple mission, in and out, but nothing ever quite worked out that way. The CIA kept tabs on Shining Path guerrillas, but they seemed to have no eyes or ears inside the group itself, no one they could reach out and touch to learn the whereabouts of one hostage in a country where guerrilla warfare had become a way of life. It took a soldier on the ground to find those contacts, squeeze them until something snapped and chase the leads he gathered all the way to payday—or the grave.

Bolan knew it could go either way, but he was in the game now, and he would be hanging tough until the final whistle blew.

His first mark was an old and seemingly abandoned block of flats on Avenida Costanera, in the Lima suburb of Callao. Its south side faced the ocean, several hundred yards away, but Bolan would be making entry from the north, by means of what appeared to be a fairly solid fire escape.

The place had been officially condemned three years earlier, but in the absence of a demolition team, the edict hadn't stopped a crowd of squatters moving in. The cops had more important things to do than rousting vagrants from abandoned buildings, and the deal looked sweet for several hundred rent-free residents...until a vanguard from the Shining Path moved in. Once the guerrillas came, it took only a day or two for word to get around. It wasn't healthy for the squatters to remain there any longer. One had fallen from the roof, while two others had their throats cut, their bodies tumbled down an open elevator shaft. Police had checked it out, removed the stiffs and issued one more round of warnings for the homeless to get out.

They could have saved their breath.

The Shining Path had achieved, within a week, what no landlord or government committee could have done in months with legal orders and decrees. The flats were emptied, with discreet graffiti warning new arrivals to look elsewhere in their search for shelter. No one lingered, argued, staged a protest march or tried to trash the place beyond its present state of disrepair.

And when the squatters had decamped, the Shining Path moved in.

They didn't fill the place. That would have been inviting trouble, begging the police or military to attack. Instead, they occupied a few strategic flats and kept the rest for dead-air storage space, an arms dump or a way station for fugitive assassins. The latest tenants threw no parties, made no noise to speak of, kept the windows painted black or blanket-draped in rooms where lanterns burned. A "junk" van parked in knee-high weeds against the west side of the building could evacuate a dozen soldiers in the case of an emergency, while other vehicles were stashed around the neighborhood, within a mile or so.

It was as good a place to start as any, even though the soldier didn't have a final head count on the occupation force and there was nothing to suggest they kept a hostage here. That would have been too easy, like a gift from heaven, and the Executioner was used to fighting hard for every inch of ground in his unending war against the savages.

This night would be no different. Death was in the air, competing with the salt smell of the ocean to the south.

It smelled like home.

MIGUEL CARDOZA TOOK his turn at guard duty like everybody else. It didn't matter that he held a rank equivalent to first lieutenant in the Shining Path; all soldiers were expected to participate in standard duties on an equal basis. It was part of what they had been fighting for, through all the bitter years.

Cardoza wasn't old enough to have participated in the early years of struggle. He had just turned twenty-five, in fact, which meant the movement had been active two full years before his birth. His father had been one of the original Shining Path soldiers, though, assassinated by the military outside Juliaca, back in 1982. By that time, young Miguel had seen and heard enough to know that he would join the movement, just as soon as he grew tall and strong enough.

He had been waging war against the government for almost seven years now, long enough to see his best friends killed and long enough for him to move up through the ranks, a combination of attrition and initiative propelling him into command of a respected fighting unit. They had staged raids in the countryside and in Iquitos, killing soldiers and police, along with those civilians who were slow and stupid when the guns went off. Cardoza had no sympathy for fools or those who loved the government that had destroyed his family, oppressed his people through long generations of abuse and exploitation. Many more would have to die before the war was won.

But not this night.

He was a simple watchdog, looking out for trouble in the run-down block of flats the Shining Path had liberated from its worthless former occupants. Cardoza wasn't expecting trouble—there had been no major challenge to their tenancy in months—but it was still a standard rule to mount a guard around the clock in case the army or municipal police closed in.

His soldiers were prepared for anything, and while the twenty-one of them would doubtless be outnumbered, they had escape plans laid out in advance—the van, a tunnel in the works—along with arms and ammunition to withstand a major siege if all else failed.

Cardoza had the ground-floor beat, while another sentry manned the stairs, one floor above him, and a third was situated on the roof, to warn of any troops or military vehicles approaching. It was an efficient system, operating on four-hour shifts, so that one three-man team would always have a full day off when they were in between guerrilla raids. At any given time, as many as one-third of his commandos—seven men in all—might be outside the block of flats, collecting information in the city, scouting future targets, taking care of private business.

Cardoza lit a cigarette and thought about the following day, *his* day off, and the woman who was waiting for his call. A married woman, six years older than Cardoza, she still had ample energy in bed, together with a fine appreciation for the younger man who found her irresistible. She also had a husband on the antiterrorism squad of the municipal police, whom she complained about in marvelous detail: his hours and assignments, his preoccupation with the job, his latest plans to foil those "vicious little bastards" of the Shining Path.

Cardoza looked forward to their meetings, both for the relief she gave him from his pent-up tensions and the wealth of information she supplied. His conduit to the police had impressed his superiors, encouraged them to think of him as a resourceful warrior, worthy of respect, perhaps consideration for an even higher rank.

And if he had to wait a little longer for his next promotion, that was—

The explosion came from somewhere in the block of flats above him, near the top. It sounded like a hand grenade, but he couldn't be sure. Already moving toward the stairs, Cardoza wondered whether someone on his team could possibly be negligent enough to set off an explosion accidentally. If not, who else could it be?

He reached the stairs and found the second sentry waiting for him on the landing, with his AK-47 braced against his hip.

"*¿Qué pasa?*" the soldier asked. *What's going on?*

"I don't know," Cardoza replied, brushing past and

starting up the next flight at a trot. "Stay here and watch below."

Before he reached the second floor, Cardoza heard the first long burst of automatic-weapons fire, still several floors above him. *That* was no accident, whatever the explosion might have been. He gripped his Kalashnikov more tightly, thumbed off the safety and held the weapon ready as he pounded up the stairs.

How could the soldiers be attacking, with no warning from his spotter on the roof? How could they be inside the building, if they hadn't gone past him downstairs?

Too many questions. He focused on the sounds of gunfire ringing in the stairwell, angry, frightened voices shouting questions back and forth as the concussive noise of combat echoed through the house.

The second floor was used for storage, so the weapons and supplies were only carried up and down two flights of stairs. No soldiers occupied that floor, but there were scattered groups on three, four, five and six. The only rules for choice of quarters in the old apartment building involved noise limits, which, Cardoza thought grimly, were clearly shot to hell by now, and common-sense restrictions on display of lights. In other circumstances, he could have recited the location of his people on each floor, but this wasn't a normal situation. From the sound of it, they were engaged in desperate battle, meaning he would have to track them down and find out what was happening.

Cardoza found four soldiers waiting for him on the third-floor landing. All of them were armed, three fully dressed, the fourth wearing only denim jeans and boots. They had the stairwell covered, leading up to four, but they weren't prepared to make the move, until Cardoza started barking orders at them, using rage and shame to urge them forward.

"Come with me!" he snapped, and they fell in behind him as he led the way upstairs.

On four, the smell of gun smoke and explosives met his nostrils. It reminded him of killing situations in the past, when he had taken the initiative against the movement's enemies. How many men were dead because of him? Cardoza had lost count, and at the moment it was totally irrelevant. He had a new fight on his hands, and there was no acceptable alternative to victory.

Another pair of soldiers joined him on the fourth floor, dressing as they left their rooms and double-timed in the direction of the stairs. The smell of blood and death assaulted them as they climbed toward the fifth-floor landing.

A haze of dust and battle smoke hung in the stairwell, and Cardoza almost stumbled on a body sprawled out on the steps. It was one of his own, although the face had been too badly damaged for a quick ID. The man was dead, and that was all that mattered at the moment.

Others would be joining him, and soon.

Cardoza paused, a few steps short of five, and glanced back to make sure none of his soldiers had deserted him. They were good men, but they had never before been attacked like this. They were accustomed to attacking others, seizing the initiative and running with the great advantage of surprise. It was a shock to have the tables turned, and he would have to watch them closely, show the kind of courage needed to defeat a lethal trap.

It was encouraging, he thought, that there was still no sound of shooting from downstairs. They might be able to escape, in spite of everything, but he wasn't prepared to run before he knew whom he was fighting and convinced himself that it was hopeless. They would have to leave the flats now, come what may, but it would be a less embarrassing retreat if he could leave a few dead enemies behind.

"Come on!" he barked again, and led the way, like any good officer would do, his finger on the trigger of his AK-47. Any second now, and he would meet the enemy. He felt the need for contact like an addict's craving.

WHEN ALL THE ODDS were stacked against him, and he knew that he could only get so far with stealth, it was a standing rule of Bolan's to begin the action with a bang. He couldn't always blitz the enemy in one fell swoop, but he could often do the next-best thing: disorient his adversaries, drop as many as he could while they were still off guard and make the rest defend themselves in chaos. It had worked before and, he reckoned, it should work again.

He entered through a sixth-floor window, cut the painted glass and reached inside to slip the latch before anyone sleeping on that floor could rouse himself and go investigate the noise. He had the Uzi submachine gun in one hand and a fragmentation grenade, minus the pin, clutched in the other as he crawled inside, prepared for any challenge from the Shining Path guerrillas he had come to kill.

And with any luck he'd have at least a few short moments to interrogate one.

It was a long shot, granted, but he had to start the action somewhere, and he could do worse than taking out a whole nest of guerrillas in a single sweep.

It looked like ten apartments occupied the sixth floor, five to either side as Bolan faced the corridor, stairs at the far end of the hall. He started forward, hearing salsa music from an open doorway on his left halfway down, drawn to the sound as evidence of adversaries now within his reach. He paused outside the open door, peered in and saw two young men rolling joints, unmindful of the fact that Death had come to call.

He took a chance, released the SMG to dangle on its shoulder strap and drew the sleek Beretta 93-R from the horizontal rig beneath his left arm, counting on the custom-fitted sound suppressor to buy a little time. He gave the door a sharp push with his right foot, checking that he hadn't missed another gunman in the flat, the slight noise making the startled hardmen lunge for their AK-47s.

Too late. Bolan took them out with two well-placed shots, holstered the Beretta and moved on. The only other flat on six that demonstrated signs of life was on his right and two doors farther down. The sound of several voices, speaking Spanish, drew him like a magnet. Once again the door was open, granting him a peek inside, where four men sat around a table, playing cards.

It was too many for the pistol: even if he tagged them all, it was a safe bet one or more would get a shot off, warn the other soldiers in the house. And if he couldn't drop them silently, it was as good a time as any to begin the fireworks.

He lobbed the frag grenade around the doorjamb, using enough force to drop it somewhere near the table. Accuracy wasn't important in a smallish room, with unprotected targets, and the bomb's five-second fuse would keep his enemies from finding decent cover, even if they saw the lethal egg in time and started to react.

The blast shook Bolan, drilling the wall above him with a dozen shrapnel holes. He rushed through the doorway seconds later, leading with the Uzi, mopping up. One of the guerrillas was on his feet, blood streaming from a ragged scalp wound, brandishing a pistol, when the Uzi spewed a stream of parabellum slugs that cut him down.

The rest were either dead or on their way, and Bolan left them where they were, intent on finding other prey.

Downstairs, he heard the other soldiers rallying, aroused from sleep or drawn away from their amusements by the sounds of combat. He was moving toward the stairs to meet them when a noise behind him stopped him short, the Uzi tracking as he turned.

A young man with an automatic rifle stood beside an open door that evidently led to a flight of stairs up to the roof. He had the rifle at his shoulder, sighting down the barrel, when a burst of parabellum manglers opened up his chest and stomach, slammed him over backward to the floor.

As Bolan reached the stairway, he could hear the soldiers massing down below, most likely working up the nerve to rush him. They would be well armed, undoubtedly with hand grenades, and he couldn't afford to let them seize the initiative. Once they began to drive him back, he would be cornered, and the fire escape would be a death trap for him, even if he made it that far toward escape.

He palmed another frag grenade and yanked the pin, lobbed the bomb downstairs and waited for the sound of the explosion. Wounded soldiers screamed, others cursing as they squeezed off aimless bursts, their bullets peppering the walls and ceiling of the stairwell.

And behind the sharp, staccato sound of automatic weapons was something else—the wail of sirens closing rapidly.

He had counted on a few more minutes, anyway, but it was probable the military and police had special flying squads on tap, with all the recent incidents, including the abduction of a high-ranked U.S. national. In any case, the last thing Bolan needed was a swarm of troops to box him in, along with his intended targets.

It was time to go.

He fired a long burst from his Uzi, catching two men on the stairs and cutting them to ribbons, bodies tumbling back and downward toward the anxious faces of their comrades. He was moving well before they hit the fifth-floor landing, back along the smoky corridor, in the direction of the open window that had been his entry hatch.

Outside, the air was cool and clean—or cleaner than the atmosphere inside a charnel house, at any rate. He scrambled down the rusty fire escape as squad cars started screeching to a halt out front. An AK-47 chattered in the street, from the direction of the sirens, telling Bolan that at least one ground-floor sentry had remained to hold the fort. With any luck, he would distract the uniforms while Bolan made his getaway.

It was a six-foot drop to reach the alley below, and the Executioner landed in a crouch, prepared for any challenge. What he got was headlights, topped by flashing blue and white, as first one squad car and then another pulled into the alley, rolling toward him with a reckless disregard for garbage bins standing in the way.

These cops meant business, and Bolan's private code prevented him from employing deadly force against them, even to preserve his life.

Which left one option open.

He would have to run like hell.

2

Captain Constantion Chavez leaned forward in his seat, with one hand on the dash, as if his posture might impart a few more miles per hour to the squad car's speed.

"Hurry up!" he snapped at the driver. "Faster!"

"Yes, Captain!"

Chavez had been at headquarters, in the Palace of Justice, when the alarm went down, explosions and shots fired at an abandoned block of flats on Avenida Costanera. The other members of his flying squad were on the street, obeying his demand for a continuous patrol by night, hoping that they could catch a band of rebels in the act, perhaps take prisoners for questioning. Chavez hadn't been counting on a full-scale battle, as described by anxious neighbors who had phoned in the report, but he would take what he could get.

The first three units of his flying squad were on the scene already, pleading urgently for reinforcements. Chavez could hear automatic weapons firing in the background and wondered what was happening. There were no targets worthy of the Shining Path in Callao—no embassies, no government offices of any kind, in fact. He couldn't understand why the guerrillas would strike there instead of at the heart of Lima, possibly his own headquarters, where their enemies abounded.

He would simply have to wait and see.

Chavez could see the flashing lights from half a mile

away, on Avenida Costanera. The police used white patrol cars for the most part, though Chavez was riding in a black unmarked sedan. He wore his Browning semiautomatic pistol in a shoulder holster, while his driver wore a normal khaki uniform and pistol belt. There was a shotgun racked beneath the front seat, automatic weapons in the trunk of the sedan, but Chavez wondered if there would be time to reach them now that they were closing on the combat zone.

He saw erratic muzzle-flashes winking from the ground-floor windows of the old apartment building, and some upstairs, as well. His men were taking cover, crouched behind their cars, already firing tear-gas canisters into the building. Chavez cursed and drew his pistol, wondering if these guerrillas would be like so many others he had dealt with in the city, outfitted with gas masks, body armor, even sandbags for the doors and windows of their headquarters.

It was now apparent that this wasn't a terrorist attack in progress. Rather, they had stumbled on a nest of gunmen, possibly with a substantial arsenal on hand. He wondered what had started the shooting in the first place, whether there had been some kind of falling-out among the terrorists, but he would have to wait for answers until they had swept the building clean.

"Turn here!" he told his driver. "Go around behind the building."

The driver did as he was told, a sharp right turn that almost pitched Chavez out of his seat. He braced one hand against the dashboard, clutched his pistol in the other as they raced a short block north and made another screeching turn, hard left this time, to come in from the rear of the apartment building.

No battle had been joined on this side of the structure yet, although a squad car was in place, its headlights zeroed on the back door to prevent the occupants from slipping out. More flashing lights reflected from an alley on the east side of the building, coming up immediately on their left. At least one squad car in the alley, then...but doing what?

Suddenly, as if in answer to the captain's silent question, a tall man appeared, bursting from the alley, head down, his knees and elbows pumping as he ran. Dressed all in black, some kind of skintight clothes beneath a military harness, he was armed with what appeared to be an Uzi submachine gun, glinting in the headlights from Chavez's squad car.

"God Almighty!"

When his driver hit the brakes, it was a reflex more than anything. They could have run the tall man down, but nothing in the driver's training had prepared him to crush suspects with his vehicle. The squad car fishtailed, Chavez gaping at the sprinter as he crossed the street in front of them. One of the officers on duty at the back door shouted a warning, then squeezed off a hasty shot that missed by yards.

Chavez assumed the runner was a member of the Shining Path: who else would be running from the old apartment building at just that moment, in the middle of a shoot-out with security police? He saw a gunman, armed and dangerous, escaping while his men stood helpless, torn between their orders to remain on station and the instinct to give chase.

"Get after him!" Chavez snapped, reaching out to punch his driver on the shoulder. "Hurry!"

The unmarked cruiser's tires smoked as they took off from a standing start in hot pursuit. The runner had already gained some fifty yards, continuing along an alleyway that opened on the far side of the street. Their headlights picked out garbage cans, but the driver followed orders, stood on the accelerator and to hell with any of the scraping, rending sounds their squad car made as it proceeded down the alley, giving chase.

Chavez would have this one himself, by God. And he planned to take him alive.

IT WAS A CLOSE THING, sprinting down the alley with two squad cars on his heels. A frag grenade or burst of parabellum shockers would have slowed them down, but Bolan wouldn't fire on lawmen, even if it meant his death or capture—one amounting to the other in a world where criminals and terrorists could strike as easily in jail as on the street. He cherished no illusions of his chances for survival if the police should corner him. Quick-trigger as they were, the very sight of Bolan's military garb and weapons might provoke a lethal fusillade, and being taken into custody would only postpone the inevitable end.

He caught a break when he was halfway down the alley, though. The point car, less than fifty feet behind him, grazed a garbage bin. The wheelman overcompensated, veering to his right with force enough to strike the wall on that side, crimp his hood and crush the prowl car's right fender in against the wheel. The second driver tried to brake in time, but he was too close, and the collision jammed the lead car sideways, blocking off the alley with a solid wedge of steel.

A pistol cracked behind him, someone trying desperately to bring him down, but Bolan ducked his head and sprinted for the alley's mouth in front of him. He could see flashers waiting for him there, reflected on the asphalt, but he had no other way to go. He put his faith in speed, picked up the pace until his lungs were burning. He cleared the alley in a headlong sprint that carried him halfway across the street before he was aware of headlights rushing toward him on the right.

The driver could have swerved a few yards and flattened Bolan in the middle of the street. Surprise or squeamishness prevented his doing so, and the screech of brakes was like giant fingernails across a chalkboard as the black sedan began to swerve.

No time to check it out or see if he was clear yet. On his left the officers crouched behind a regulation squad car spotted him, one of them shouting at him and squeezing off a shot before he had a chance to aim. The bullet sizzled past its target, as Bolan weaved slightly as he ran to throw the shooter off. It was a tactic that could backfire, if they opened up on him with automatic weapons, but he had only a few more yards to go before he gained the temporary cover of another alleyway across the street.

A second shot came closer, still a foot or more to Bolan's left. He zigzagged one last time, then plunged into the darkness of the alley, grateful for the cover while it lasted, knowing that it wouldn't be for long.

The black sedan came after him, tires squealing on the turn, its high beams lighting up the alley like a noonday sun. He didn't bother running serpentine in those constricted quarters, knowing that a lucky ricochet could find him just as easily as any well-aimed shot. Behind him, closing rapidly, he heard the chase car scraping rusty bumpers, slamming into garbage cans, no replay of the lucky accident that had protected him brief moments earlier. This driver knew his stuff and didn't seem to mind the damage he was doing to his vehicle. Unless a fallen trash can jammed the chase car's wheels somehow, they had a decent chance of catching him in seconds.

The rusty ladder for another fire escape was coming at him on his left, and there was no time to see if it would hold his weight. Bolan leaped with outstretched hands, the Uzi swinging on its shoulder strap and banging painfully against his ribs. He caught the ladder's lower rung and twisted in midair, legs rising until Bolan's knees were level with his chest. He squinted in the headlights' glare and hung on for dear life, afraid the driver might be quick enough to stop and leave him dangling there, a perfect target for their guns.

But the black sedan kept rolling, startled faces gaping at him through the windshield. When the car was directly underneath him, Bolan let go of the ladder, dropped onto the roof of the sedan and clung there, like a gecko sunning on a rock.

The car was slowing, but there was only so much brakes could do to counteract momentum in the space of thirty feet. They cleared the alley's mouth, tires screaming, and the car swung broadside, flinging Bolan from his perch.

He hit the pavement running, nearly lost his balance, saved it with an outstretched hand. His other hand was clamped around a cylinder that dangled from his combat harness, jerking free the smoke grenade, unpinning it. A power pitch lobbed it through the driver's open window. It glanced off his headrest and tumbled to the floor behind his seat.

It blew four seconds later, spewing out a dense white smoke that would eventually fill an area of fifteen thousand cubic feet. There was no shrapnel, no explosion, but the smoke would blind the driver and his passenger as long as they remained inside the car.

It should have been enough, but Bolan took no chances. He was off and running by the time the cruiser's doors swung open, bodies tumbling to the pavement, racked with coughing fits.

He sprinted for the next street over, eastbound, hoping he could reach his vehicle and get away from there before he had to deal with any reinforcements.

MIGUEL CARDOZA FIRED another short burst from his AK-47 at the policemen below. He couldn't tell if anyone was hit, as most of them were crouched behind their squad cars, but shooting made him feel like he was doing something, not just sitting back and waiting for the ax to fall.

His sniper's nest was on the third floor of the old apartment building. Cordoza had worked his way downstairs, once they had lost the stranger up on six. The greater threat right now came from the security police, who had already cut off all retreat.

Cardoza risked a glance outside and saw one of the officers emerging from behind his car. He had a tear-gas gun, the short stock braced against his shoulder as he aimed. Cardoza strafed him with a burst from the Kalashnikov and saw him stagger backward, firing his projectile into the sky. It fell to earth among his comrades seconds later, and exploded in a cloud of drifting, choking fumes.

Poetic justice, Cardoza thought. They liked gas so much, they could breathe it for a while.

Still, it was but a temporary respite, and the sounds of gunfire barely slackened on the street. Cardoza checked the AK-47's magazine and found it almost empty. He dropped it, took a fresh one from his pocket and rammed it home. At least now, when he made his move, he would be ready to defend himself.

His only hope of getting out was a break across the rooftops, if he had the skill to pull it off. Cardoza couldn't take the others with him, even if they had the nerve to try. More men would only slow him down, increase the chances that he would be caught or killed. It was a high risk, even by himself, but he would have to take the chance.

Cardoza stepped back from the window, careful not to make himself a target as he started moving toward the stairs. One of the others saw him.

"Miguel, where are you going?"

"We need ammunition," he replied.

"I'll help you fetch it."

"No! Stay there and watch the pigs. I won't be long."

The ammunition was downstairs, on two, but no one saw him take the next flight up, thigh muscles burning as he took the stairs three at a time, hunched forward in a rush. Two of his men lay crumpled on the fourth-floor landing, where their bodies had come to rest after the hand grenade went off among them, on the stairs leading to five. The blast had scorched Cardoza's clothing, singed his eyebrows, but he had escaped the shrapnel. If he was a praying man, Cardoza would have said it was a miracle. In any case, he knew he was damned lucky, and he didn't mean to waste that luck by standing fast against such hopeless odds.

The Shining Path didn't need another martyr. It would be much better, all around, if he could slip away and carry a report to his superiors about the evening's strange events. Of course, in his report Cardoza would acquire a more heroic aspect than his actions otherwise might warrant. Who could blame him if he dressed the story up a bit to help himself?

What mattered was alerting his fellow soldiers to this new threat: a man in black who came from nowhere, striking like some evil wraith and slipping out again, before they had a chance to bring him down. Cardoza reckoned the arrival of security police was a coincidence, though he couldn't be certain. Better minds than his, of higher rank, could puzzle over that, once he had reported in.

But first he had to make his getaway.

On six, he moved past open doors, saw bodies sprawled out in the smoky flats. Another door stood open on the staircase leading to the roof. Ricardo Vega lay faceup in a spreading pool of blood. How many of his soldiers had the stranger killed?

No matter. They would all be dead before the pigs were finished. All except Cardoza, if his hasty scheme paid off.

He made it to the roof and paused there for a moment, breathing in the night air that wasn't yet tainted with a pall of gun smoke. He could hide up there, but they would seek him out when they had finished with the others down below.

He crossed the roof and peered down at the next rooftop in line, some twelve to fifteen feet below him. The construction crew hadn't supplied a ladder for him, and he had to drop his rifle, since it had no shoulder sling, remembering to set the safety first. Cardoza crawled over backward until he could dangle by his hands, the drop reduced by something close to half when he let go. It jarred his kidneys, even so, and spiked one ankle with a vicious pain.

Cardoza cursed and retrieved his weapon, hobbling rapidly across that roof to reach the next one, sounds of combat growing smaller with each step he took.

IN NORMAL CIRCUMSTANCES, at a walking pace Mack Bolan would have reached his car within five minutes, but he was stalled by the police and military vehicles that kept responding to the shooting call. He didn't bother counting, after he was driven into darkened doorways for the third time in the space of thirty seconds, knowing he had to find another way to travel if he wanted to survive.

And so it was that Bolan chose the same route as his enemy, Miguel Cardoza, although he was moving in the opposite direction, eastward from the battle site. It was a relatively easy move, once Bolan reached another alley, memory informing him that seven buildings lay between him and the next street, where his car was parked. The rooftop route was slower, with its varied obstacles, but its attraction was the absence of police.

So far, at least.

He slipped into the alley just as two more squad cars and a flatbed truck with soldiers sitting in the back rolled past. One of the drivers flashed a spotlight on the littered passageway as they drove by, but Bolan ducked behind a leaky garbage bin, breathing in the stench of rotting food.

The fire escape he chose was rusty, coming loose in places, but it bore his weight. He climbed past windows that were lighted now, despite the hour, the occupants roused from sleep by battle sounds and sirens. No one saw him pass; most of them kept their flimsy curtains closed on bedroom windows, but he picked up worried-sounding voices here and there along the way.

Afraid of terrorists, or the authorities? he wondered. In Peru, the violence cut both ways. Police and military officers were known to have a blank check, more or less, in dealing with a threat from terrorists. Peru had thrown off military rule in 1980, but a host of problems—with the Shining Path prominent among them—had prompted the president to dissolve the National Congress twelve years later, suspending inconvenient sections of the constitution and inaugurating widespread censorship. The latest almanacs described Peru's government as "in transition." It might not be totalitarian, but it would do until a strong man came along.

The roof was flat and filthy, soiled by years of air pollution and the leavings of the lower-income families who lived downstairs. Some of them dumped their trash up there, despite the fact that it would have been easier to toss it out a window to the alleyway below.

There were no gaps between the rooftops Bolan crossed, but some of them were different heights, requiring him to jump or climb from one roof to another. Sometimes there were ladders; sometimes not. He carried fifty feet of slender nylon rope for such emergencies, and it had served him well before he traveled half the distance to his car.

At last, when he had reached the final rooftop, Bolan checked the street below and found no squad cars waiting for him. They hadn't blocked off the neighborhood as yet.

He had a chance.

But he couldn't climb down from where he stood. The building seemed to have no fire escape, and whether that was simple negligence or a deliberate oversight, it made no difference at the moment. He could use his rope and scramble down the west wall, as vulnerable as an insect on a windowpane before he had to jump the last twelve feet...or he could go inside.

The rooftop access door hadn't been locked since someone pried the bolt off long ago. The tenants didn't care: it wasn't *their* roof, and a burglar desperate enough to raid such humble dwellings would inevitably find a way inside, regardless of locked doors.

The stairway smelled like garlic, cheese and urine all mixed up into a scent that would gag a maggot. Bolan held his breath at first, then started breathing through his mouth to beat the odor, but enough got through to make him hurry.

He cleared six floors without encountering a tenant of the house. Downstairs he checked the street in both directions prior to stepping through the door. His combat garb and weapons would betray him instantly if he was seen, but the alternative was walking down the street stark naked and unarmed.

No choice at all.

His car was close enough that he could see it now, within a hundred feet of where he stood. The only way to reach it was to get out there and make the hike, with all the risks attached.

He took a deep breath, held it, then let the door swing shut behind him, moving like Death's shadow through the night.

3

Captain Chavez stood on the sidewalk fronting Avenida Costanera, watching as the stretcher teams brought corpses from the old apartment building and lined them up along the curb. They had eleven dead so far, not counting two policemen killed and one who had lost so much blood before the ambulance arrived that he would almost surely die.

How many more inside?

A walking tour of the "abandoned" house made Chavez think they would find six or seven more at least. Security police and soldiers had already searched the place for live ones, and had come up empty. There was no one left to talk about the cause of what had happened here this night. There was one living witness that he knew of, and Chavez himself had let the man escape.

His eyes still smarted from the smoke grenade, and he had spent the past half hour coughing, wondering if he could ever get the smell out of his suit. They should have run the bastard down or shot him in the back. It would look bad in his report, an error that could bring a reprimand from his superiors.

"A pretty shooting match you've had tonight."

Chavez could only grimace as he recognized the voice of Major Serafin Padilla. It wasn't enough to be embarrassed, saddled with the chore of sorting corpses all night long; now he would have to treat this fascist bully with the proper military courtesy, pretend that they hadn't despised each other from the first time they were introduced.

"Good evening, Major. We've controlled the situation, I believe."

"I'll be the judge of that."

Padilla moved along the line of corpses, peering into twisted, bloodstained faces. When he came back to Chavez, his thin lips curled into a sneering smile.

"You've made a fair dent in the Shining Path, anyway," the major said.

"Some of these men were dead before we got here," Chavez told him, knowing he should keep his mouth shut, save it all for his report. Still, there was something in Padilla's attitude and manner that provoked him.

"Oh?"

"It was a citizen's report of gunfire and explosions that resulted in our coming here tonight. It may be that the rebels had a falling-out among themselves, or these men may be members of two rival groups. We don't know yet."

"These *men*," Padilla answered, "are traitors to their country. They have paid the price. What difference does it make who pulled the trigger?"

"It makes all the difference in the world," Chavez replied, "if the Shining Path is divided to the point of members killing one another. It could mean more trouble."

"Or perhaps a golden opportunity," Padilla said. "Let this scum kill its own kind for a while, instead of decent citizens. Our job is that much easier, when we take care of the survivors."

Chavez made no reply. It was a well-known fact that several members of Padilla's unit had been charged with murder, torture and assorted other crimes, before the amnesty on human-rights offenses set them free. There were persistent rumors that the major kept in touch with those who left the force under a cloud, helped organize them into "supplemental" death squads, then unleashed them on a list of enemies that wasn't limited to members of the Shining Path. No one had managed to indict the major, because his troops were loyal and he left no civilian witnesses to his more brutal and outrageous crimes. How many peasants he had slaughtered in the countryside, no one could say.

"I understand one of the bastards got away," Padilla said.

"Yes, sir."

There was no point denying it; he had already issued a description of the fugitive, as best he could, and it would all be written down in his report.

"*You* lost him, I believe," Padilla added.

"I did." Chavez made no excuses; they would only give Padilla further grounds for shaming him before his men.

"That was most careless of you, Captain. You agree?"

"Yes, sir."

"You lost how many men tonight?" Padilla asked.

"Two dead," Chavez replied. "Three wounded, one of whom is critical."

"And those men died while you were chasing *one* man, who eluded you. Is that correct?"

Chavez felt angry color rising in his cheeks. "The officers were shot before I reached the scene."

"None after?"

"No, sir."

"It's a pity that you didn't get here sooner, Captain."

There was no correct response to that, and Chavez offered none. He stood and watched the line of corpses growing on the sidewalk. Fourteen bodies, now, with more to come.

"There may be repercussions over this," Padilla said. "Of course, I'll put a word in for you, if I can."

And he would twist the knife, Chavez thought. What he said was, "Thank you, sir."

"It's nothing, Captain. We're all in this war together, after all."

With that, the major turned and walked back to his car. Chavez stared after him and wondered why, if they were all in it together, he should feel so terribly alone.

MAJOR PADILLA DIDN'T GIVE a damn about the one who got away. A stray guerrilla, more or less, was nothing to inspire concern. The country teemed with enemies: subversives, leftists, liberals, meddling priests, investigative journalists from other countries. They were all lined up against the state, each one of them another reason why democracy had failed in 1992, why it would always fail, until the people of Peru accepted law and order in their lives, the way they now accepted Jesus or the Shining Path.

There was no trick to keeping order, in Padilla's view. You simply made rules and enforced them strictly, without fear or favor. Anyone who broke the law had to be punished, beaten down until they learned humility, obedience and the appropriate respect. Those who resisted served, in death, as clear examples of the retribution that was waiting for subversives, rebels, terrorists and scofflaws.

It meant nothing to Padilla that he had been criticized for his techniques by various outsiders—Communists, Utopians, the kind of useless bleeding hearts whose policies had led to anarchy in the United States and Western Europe. He cared nothing for the fact that he was singled out, by name, in various reports from Amnesty International. The Shining Path guerrillas labeled him a

butcher—El Carnicero—and he wore the label like a
badge of honor. He would happily be judged by those
who called themselves his enemies.

Not everyone agreed with his techniques, of course.
Captain Chavez was one who looked askance at any use
of force beyond "the minimum required" to stabilize a
given situation. Weaklings of his kind had done their best
to undermine the rule of law and order in Peru, parading
for "democracy," when what they really wanted was a
license to ignore the rules of civilized society. Padilla
dealt with them as if they were mentally impaired, waiting
patiently until their own pathetic failings tripped them up.
Sometimes, with luck, he found an opportunity to help
them on their way.

Chavez, for instance, with his bungled effort to arrest
one of the terrorists that night. It was amusing, when he
thought about it. Not enough for a demotion or dismissal,
maybe not enough to rate a formal reprimand, but it would
go into the captain's file and fester there, perhaps denying
him promotion, weighing in if he made any more mistakes
along the way.

The captain had tried to undermine Padilla in the past.
No overt challenges, which would have brought him to a
court-martial, but there was a constant undertone of crit-
icism, orders countermanded on occasion, always with
some logical excuse.

The raid on Agua Verde, twelve months earlier, had
been a case in point. Padilla knew the residents of Agua
Verde were collaborators with the Shining Path. He knew
this in his heart, because they shared no information with
his troops, when there were plainly rebels in the neighborhood, and outlawed weapons had been found among
their huts on more than one occasion. Granted, those con-
sisted of an ancient shotgun and a rusty .38 revolver, but

the very paucity of solid evidence convinced Padilla of their guile.

Padilla had decided that the village should be used as an example to the law-abiding peasants of the province, warn them of the danger of cooperating with the Communists before they made the same mistakes. He issued orders for a sweep that would have razed the village, relocated or imprisoned its inhabitants and executed on the spot any who dared resist. It was to be a standard operation, of the sort that he had carried out a hundred times before...until Chavez had intervened.

Padilla wasn't present when the sweep went forward. He had sent a first lieutenant and a force of fifty men to do the job. Unknown to him, Chavez had seen the orders somehow and was waiting, with his own men, when Padilla's force arrived. The young lieutenant was outranked, his men outnumbered; he had joined Chavez in yet another search of Agua Verde, which, predictably, had turned up nothing. Padilla bit his tongue and transferred the lieutenant to a rural district where the last four officers in charge had been assassinated by Shining Path gunmen.

He said nothing whatsoever to Chavez.

Two weeks later, when a crack civilian death squad swept the village, Chavez wasn't lurking in the bushes to protect the traitors. They had been annihilated to a man. So would it always be, for those who stood against the righteous power of the state.

There had been ugly rumors in the past about Padilla's failure to investigate the so-called crimes of wealthy businessmen—the miners, brewers, timber cutters, ranchers and narcotics dealers who exerted heavy influence in Lima. Some of them were said to practice human sacrifice, and all were branded as corrupt by those who never understood the proper role of government. Padilla understood the state's role in Peru: it was to guarantee the national security against subversives and suppress the spread of communism, even now that Russia was defunct and Castro was a senile joke. The threat remained, as it had always been, a clear and present danger to an orderly society.

As for the rest, those economic "crimes" that so outraged the liberal bleeding hearts, Padilla had no time for persecuting men who were the very backbone of society. He wasn't paid to stir up scandals that provided rebels like the Shining Path with further propaganda for their lying tabloids. The police could always deal with minor violations of the civil law, once they had won the civil war that had been savaging Peru for better than a quarter century.

He could remember when the trouble started, two short years before he joined the army and proceeded on from there to the security police. His older sister had been walking home from school the afternoon a car bomb rocked their neighborhood in Puerto Maldonado. There was nothing left of her to bury but a pair of blackened shoes. From that day forward, he had watched his family come apart, his father drinking, while his mother never really found her way back from the graveyard where his sister's funeral was held. Her own death, three years later, from a "wasting illness" doctors were unable to define, had been another strike against the rebels, in Padilla's mind. He had been motivated from the day of his enlistment in the military by a need for vengeance, growing over time into the granite-hard philosophy that ruled his life.

Disrupters of society had to pay. No one was truly innocent; each man and woman harbored the malignant virus of rebellion somewhere in their hearts. It was Padilla's job—his holy mission—to eradicate those who gave in to the disease, and in the process to persuade its hapless carriers, the great mass of society, that they were better off suppressing any urge to turn against the state.

Captain Chavez, by contrast, was a man who spoke of "freedom" as if it were some God-given right, instead a privilege earned by hard work and devotion to duty. He would fail, in time, because of that inherent weakness, and Padilla was determined that his failure should come sooner rather than later.

He was glad to give Chavez a strong shove toward retirement from the service. Failing that, and if the captain saw fit to defy his betters, then Padilla might arrange to drop him in a grave.

Peru was overrun with graveyards, many of them hidden in the countryside, unrecognized by any but the chosen few who made deposits to the soil from time to time. Padilla could dispose of Chavez, given time and provocation. It would be a relatively simple thing.

But first he had reports to file, a few tricks up his sleeve. The death card was a last resort, but it would always be there, waiting for him in a pinch.

A part of him hoped that Chavez would make a fight of it, give him the one excuse he needed to take firm, decisive action on his own. It would be pleasant, he imagined, to obliterate that smirking face.

The notion kept him smiling all the way back to his office, through the hour he spent typing his report. Much later, when he finally lay down to sleep, his dreams were full of fire and blood.

MIGUEL CARDOZA FELT undressed without his AK-47, but the small .380 pistol in his pocket made him feel a little better as he walked the streets of Lima, dodging late police patrols and looking for a public telephone.

It was a modern city; phones were everywhere. His problem was that most of them were situated in the lobbies of assorted businesses, and it was too late—or early, depending on your point of view—for any of those shops and offices to be found open. He had walked for miles, it seemed, although he realized his hypervigilance and paranoia may have made the trek seem longer than it was.

One thing he knew for sure was that the pigs were out in force. They would have no description of him—there was nothing back at the apartment building to give them his identity—but the Peruvian security police weren't averse to stopping anyone they saw, for questioning. If that should happen, and they frisked him, found a pistol in his pocket, he would certainly be jailed. It hardly mattered if they linked him to the shoot-out. It wasn't unknown for the Peruvian police to frame a suspect, and the simple weapons charge carried a penalty of five years by itself. He had no automatic right to call a lawyer, which, in turn, meant that it could be days, or even weeks, before his brothers of the Shining Path found out he was in custody. He wouldn't have a chance to tell his version of the firefight, what had happened with the man in black, before it was too late.

That much was settled, then. If a patrol car stopped him, he would have to kill the officers inside before they had a chance to search him. Even as the thought was formed, Cardoza stepped into a shadowed doorway, took the semi-auto pistol from his pocket, cocked and locked it, slipping it inside his waistband, at the front, where it was covered by his shirttail.

Better.

He resumed his long search for a telephone, muttering curses as he passed the plate-glass windows of a dozen shops or offices with wall phones mounted just beyond his reach. Another three blocks, and he reached a service station, also closed, but here the telephone was mounted on a metal post outside.

Whom to call?

The only name that came to mind was Pirro Lopez. He commanded Shining Path's troops in Lima, and while he had spoken to Cardoza no more than two or three times in his life, he was the only ranking officer the young man could think of who possessed a telephone. It would be worth disturbing him at this late hour, to inform him of the shoot-out and the loss of life. Cardoza couldn't be certain all his men were dead, of course, but it was probable. They were indoctrinated with the risks of being taken prisoner, and the security police on Avenida Costanera were in no mood to negotiate surrender.

He had worked a story out, while he was running, and he hoped that his superiors would buy it. In the new, improved rendition, he had chased the man in black across the rooftops by himself, but had to let him go when the police arrived in force. He had turned back to help his comrades, but the building was surrounded. It was certain death, with nothing gained, for him to join the fight.

The story had a ring of truth, and it should stand, as long as there was no one to dispute him. Even then, half his men were down before the pigs arrived, and only five—all dead but one, when he escaped—knew positively that he hadn't chased the black-clad stranger from the building.

Good enough.

He dropped the coins into the telephone and tapped out Lopez's number, frowning as a busy signal grated on his nerves. Whom could Lopez be talking to at this hour of the night?

He cradled the receiver, fished his change out of the coin-return slot, thinking. Someone else had heard about the firefight, and was calling in the news. No problem. It couldn't be anyone from *his* team; all of them were either dead or locked up in a cell by now. Some secondhand report, then. Lopez would be grateful for an update, and Cardoza didn't have to concern himself with waking him if the man was up and talking on the telephone.

He tried again. Still busy.

He couldn't loiter at the telephone, in case another squad car came around and spotted him. Disgusted, anxious, jumpy, he decided that the best thing he could do was take a walk around the block, give Lopez time to finish with his other call and try again in ten or fifteen minutes. He could play that game until the sun came up, if necessary, but Cardoza knew his nerves would be scraped raw by then.

No matter.

With another curse, he stuck the coins in his pocket, checked the pistol in his belt and set off walking through the darkness, going nowhere.

THE NAME of Pirro Lopez had a star beside it on the checklist Bolan carried in his head. Rumored to be the second-in-command of the Shining Path since the shakeup back in 1992, when the authorities picked off the movement's founder and a number of his ranking aides. The rest was history, and Lopez was supposed to be one of the slickest cats around, able to come and go in Lima as he pleased, residing there when he wasn't out in the field and keeping up his playboy image under any one of several pseudonyms.

A contract agent for the CIA had stumbled on his Lima love nest, more or less by accident, and the address had been confirmed, but Langley held it back from the Peruvian police for reasons of their own. Bolan wasn't concerned about their motives. At the moment all he cared about was meeting Pirro Lopez for a little one-on-one.

The house, located two blocks north of Avenida Bolivar, was neither large nor lavish in appearance, but it had a wooden fence around three sides, left open at the front. A drive-by confirmed sentries in an old sedan out front, and Bolan drove around the block to come in from the alley at the rear.

There was no watchdog in the yard, no sign of any other lookouts or security devices. The two guns in front were Lopez's early-warning system, but he obviously felt secure enough in Lima to refrain from traveling with a whole retinue of bodyguards.

His first mistake.

Bolan was over the fence and across the yard in nothing flat. He checked the back door for alarms before he picked the lock. The kitchen had a fast-food smell about it, but he didn't linger to investigate. Instead, he checked the empty living room, then moved along a hallway leading to the bedrooms, two of them, located at the west end of the house.

He heard the woman's voice when he was halfway to the nearest bedroom door, her words inaudible, despite a tone of urgency. He peered around the doorjamb, saw her naked back and buttocks as she straddled the chest of a man whose feet were pointed toward the doorway. She was leaning forward, speaking to him rapidly in Spanish.

Bolan stepped into the room and moved to one side of the door, just far enough that he could glimpse the man's face. Dark eyes were open wide, but he wouldn't have pegged the look as rampant lust. If anything, it looked like fear.

He cleared his throat, and the woman swiveled to face him, making no attempt to hide her nakedness. She kept one hand at Lopez's throat, a shiny knife blade glinting in the pale light from a bedside lamp. She saw the Beretta and didn't seem to care. Her Spanish, when she spoke, was rapid-fire and fluent.

"Sorry," Bolan said, "I didn't follow that."

She blinked at him, surprised now, but she kept a firm grip on the knife. "I said, if you take one more step, I'll cut his throat."

"I'd like to have a few words with him first, if you don't mind."

That made her frown, a beat of hesitation, while she tossed her head to clear the dark hair from her face. The movement made her breasts sway slightly, a distraction Bolan might have focused on in other circumstances.

Not this time.

"Who are you?" she demanded.

"Let's just say I dropped in uninvited, for a chat with Señor Lopez there."

"You'll have to get in line," she said.

"I wouldn't argue, normally," he told her, "with a view like that." She blushed, bright color rising in her cheeks, as if she hadn't noticed she was naked until now. "Unfortunately," he continued, "I'm a little short of time. Are you aware your playmate's got two goons outside?"

"So what?"

"I have a hunch they may get curious when you walk out of here without their boss."

"I'll take my chances."

"Fair enough, but I still need to have a word with him, before you go to work."

"I told you—"

Bolan raised the pistol higher. "Sorry. I insist."

"You'd shoot a naked woman?"

"Only as a last resort," he told her, "and with great regret."

She rocked back on her haunches, then, considering her options. She still held the blade to Lopez's throat, but he had picked up on her hesitation, maybe felt the slightest relaxation of the pressure underneath his chin, and knew that it was now or never.

Bucking with his hips and twisting at the same time, Lopez grabbed the woman's wrist and hauled her to the left, his right, so that her body rose between him and the pistol Bolan held, spine arched, legs splayed. She tried to keep her balance, but Lopez swung his free hand in a roundhouse punch that caught her on the cheek and dumped her to the floor beside the bed. No sooner was he free than Lopez made a lunge to reach the top drawer of the nightstand, yanked it open, scrabbling around inside.

It had to be a gun, Bolan thought, but he still held off on shooting Lopez, hoping he could yet disarm the guy and make him talk. He was about to rush the bed, in fact, when the woman staggered to her feet and lurched a short step backward, blocking him.

And Lopez had his weapon now, a shiny automatic pistol, thumbing back the hammer as he twisted on the bed to find a target. Squeezing off the first shot in a rush, he missed both adversaries, and the bullet whispered over Bolan's head.

There was no time to grapple with him now, no hope of grilling him before the echo of his gunshot brought the outside sentries running to his aid. The 93-R stuttered, spitting out a silent 3-round burst, and Lopez vaulted backward, slamming against the headboard, as the parabellum shockers drilled his chest.

"You killed him, you...you..."

Sputtering with rage, the woman turned on Bolan. She still held the knife, but made no move to use it, while he kept the 93-R leveled at her navel.

"Who the hell—?"

"No time for that," he interrupted her, already fading back to one side of the door as he heard Lopez's watchdogs coming. He was ready when they bulled in through the bedroom doorway, stopping short and gaping at the woman for a crucial moment, then refocusing on Lopez, crumpled on the bed.

With the Beretta switched to semiautomatic, Bolan stroked the trigger twice and dropped them where they stood, clean head shots. They went down together in a heap, and lay unmoving on the bloodstained carpet.

"I'm leaving now," he told the woman, making no real effort to avert his gaze. "If you need a ride, it's time to grab your clothes and get a move on."

"Wait a second!"

"No. It's now or never."

Bolan turned and left the bedroom, moving through the silent house to exit by the same way he had entered. He was halfway to the fence before he heard the woman following, a steady stream of curses spewing from her lips as she tried dressing on the run.

"Will you slow down?"

He scaled the fence without a backward glance and moved off toward his vehicle. The woman had some difficulty with the wood fence, climbing over in her panties, carrying her dress and shoes. Rough gravel in the alley gouged her feet, but she was running by the time she reached the car and climbed in on the driver's side.

He sat still for a moment, watching all that scenery disappear as she began to put the dress on, pulling it over her head. She caught him at it, scowling as she slipped into her high-heeled shoes.

"Show's over, guy," she told him. "Are we getting out of here or what?"

He put the car in gear and drove into the night.

4

They were driving west on Avenida Argentina, cruising aimlessly, when Bolan broke the silence that had hung between them like a soundproof curtain for the past five minutes.

"You can start explaining anytime," he said.

"You first." The woman's voice was firm, no quavering.

"It doesn't play that way," he told her. "I was after Lopez on official business. You got in the way and screwed it up. You might have blown things altogether. If I drop you at the U.S. Embassy, the very least you can expect will be a one-way ticket home, assuming the security police don't put a bid in for you, first."

"And why would they be looking for me?"

"Somebody could make a call. You never know."

"You bastard!"

"Save the flattery. Let's start off with your name, and go from there."

She thought about it for another moment, staring out the window, then her shoulders slumped, the body language of defeat.

"It's Mercy Hastings."

Bolan clutched the steering wheel a little tighter, waiting for the tight knot in his stomach to dissolve. The name could hardly be coincidence. He knew most of the story in a flash, like that, before the woman spoke again.

"You know that Lopez was a member of the Shining Path, I guess," she said. "A ranking officer, in fact."

"That wasn't common knowledge," Bolan replied.

"One thing I've never been accused of is being common."

And he recognized the truth in that, right off the top. "Go on," he prompted.

"My father is a senior secretary with the embassy in Lima. Garrick Hastings. Does it ring a bell?"

Alarm bells. "Keep talking."

"He was kidnapped seven days ago by members of the Shining Path. They claimed responsibility, the usual. No reason to assume they're lying."

"So?"

"So, when I couldn't get a furlough, I went AWOL from my post at Benning—"

"That's *Fort* Benning?" Bolan interrupted her.

"Affirmative." She cracked a smile, enjoying his surprise. "I'm in my second tour. They had us in for a refresher course at jump school."

"And you took a hike."

"Damned straight. Nobody else was getting off his ass to find my father. Every day these bastards hold him bumps the odds against them freeing him alive."

He knew the truth of that. It had inspired the urgency of his assignment, when the word came down to Stony Man from Pennsylvania Avenue.

"And you have some idea that you can get him back alone?"

"I made it this far," she replied defiantly. "I'd know where they were holding him by now, except for your John Wayne impression."

"How'd you get to Lopez?" Bolan asked.

"I started with my father's mistress. Miranda Muñoz.

Don't look so surprised," she said. "My mother died five years ago. We all have needs."

"What happened with the lady?" Bolan asked, already certain of the answer.

"Gone. Officially the local cops don't know if she was kidnapped with my father, or if she was in on it. I'm betting on the second choice."

"Which brings us back to Lopez," Bolan said.

"I get around," she told him. "People talk."

"They sell you out, too."

"I was careful. Anyway, I found out who he was and where he likes to strut his stuff. I made myself available. It worked…almost, that is. Until you came along."

"Were you prepared to kill him?"

"Absolutely."

"I suspect the best thing you can do right now is head back to the States and try to talk your way out of a court-martial."

"Forget it, mister. Take me to the embassy, if that's your best shot, but I guarantee, if they put me on a plane, I'll turn around and come right back."

"It could be tough without a passport."

"I'm resourceful."

And he could believe that, too.

"The thing is," Bolan said, "I've been assigned to find your father."

"Oh, terrific. I feel *so* much better now."

"You've been how long in uniform?"

"Three years," she said. "What of it?"

"You should know enough to leave a tough job to professionals."

"So, what about Lopez?" she challenged him.

"I would have picked his brain by now, if Mata Hari hadn't gotten in the way."

"You think so?"

"Bottom line," Bolan said, "you don't know the country or the opposition. I'm prepared to bet you've never killed a man. The last thing I need at the moment is an untrained tagalong who's got outstanding warrants in the States."

"Untrained! I'll have you know—"

"This isn't jump school," Bolan interrupted. "It isn't Desert Storm. This game is down and dirty from the time you ante in."

"So, it's a game to you."

"Figure of speech," he said. "Winners and losers, anyway, except the losers don't go home and bitch about it afterward."

Hastings was silent for a block or so, and when she spoke again, her voice was on the edge of breaking. Bolan guessed he would have seen a glint of tears if he had glanced at her just then, and he kept both eyes on the road.

"They have my father, dammit! If you'd ever lost—"

"I have." His voice was graveyard flat and stony cold.

Another moment passed before she asked him, "Have you got a name?"

"Belasko. Mike."

"Okay, Belasko Mike. What are you? Delta Force? The CIA?"

"What difference does it make?"

"To me? Not one damned bit if you can bring my father back alive."

"That was the plan."

"I still think I can help you, though," she said.

"I'll bet."

"I'm serious. It's true, I've only had three days in Lima, but I speak the language, and I *did* find Lopez, right?"

He had to give her that much, anyway. And she had

managed it without support from the intelligence community. Still, there was no way he could justify inserting Mercy Hastings into front-line combat with the Shining Path, while he was hunting for her father. That would be the capper, bringing Garrick Hastings back to find his daughter dead.

No way. If he could only stall her long enough to set a pickup, it could still work out.

"There may be something you can do," he said at last.

"I'm listening."

"Intelligence collection. I have to think about it for a while, to nail the right approach."

"So, what's 'a while'?"

"Two hours, maybe three. Where are you staying?"

"Why?" she asked, suspicion creeping back into her voice.

"I need to know where I can find you, right? If I need you, and you're out there on the street somewhere, we might as well forget it."

"The Hotel Obregon," she said. "On Avenida Uruguay."

"What name?" he asked her.

"I just told you—"

"What name did you use to *register*."

"Oh. My own. The MPs won't be looking for me here. Besides, I had to show my passport when I checked in, and I don't have spares."

He had already changed his course, homing on Avenida Uruguay. "I want your promise that you'll wait for me," he said, "and not go running off alone."

"Three hours?" she asked him.

"Tops."

"Okay, agreed. And what will you be doing in the meantime?"

Bolan's smile would have unnerved the devil.

"I think," he said, "it's time to give the Shining Path a wake-up call."

CAPTAIN CHAVEZ was working on the first draft of his field report as dawn broke over Lima. He was setting down the facts in longhand, prior to typing them in triplicate, already wondering what kind of spin he ought to put on the report. Major Padilla would be out to undermine him, and he couldn't hide the fact that he had let a fugitive escape.

If it had been Padilla writing the report, Chavez thought, he would make it sound as if a major battle had been won against the Shining Path. And it was true, since the final body count of eighteen terrorists couldn't be ranked as insignificant. Chavez's problem, simply stated, was that he was certain his men were responsible for barely half those kills, if that.

His walk-through at the shooting scene had shown him evidence of fighting on the upper floors, including two or more grenade blasts that hadn't occurred after police arrived. In fact, he knew it was the sound of gunfire and explosions in the building that had prompted neighbors to request help in the first place. As for the man who got away...

It was a risky thing to generalize, the captain knew, particularly on the flimsiest of evidence, but even in the darkness, driving hell-bent down a narrow alley, there had still been time for certain observations. First the man who had eluded him that night was taller than the average Peruvian by at least six or seven inches. His garb and gear, from what Chavez had seen, were wholly inconsistent with the clothing worn by terrorists in the apartment building. And, finally, Chavez had glimpsed his face—first when the man had leaped up on the fire escape, before he dropped onto Chavez's car, and then again when he rolled off, for a split second, prior to the explosion of his smoke grenade.

It was enough. Chavez was ready, under oath, to say the man was white, American or European. But he was frankly hesitant to break the news in his report.

It was embarrassing enough that he had lost the man, been smoked out of his own patrol car, and he knew Padilla's field report would focus on those facts as much as possible, while building up the major's nonexistent role in the engagement. What would Chavez gain by telling his superiors that it had been a white man who eluded him? Padilla and some others would insist he was deluded, even lying. They were focused on the long war with the Shining Path, to the exclusion of all else. A stranger in the city, killing native terrorists for unknown reasons, would make no sense to the army or security police. The Shining Path guerrillas weren't drug traffickers, after all, with rival syndicates intent on seizing merchandise or territory.

No. It simply made no sense...but he couldn't deny what he had seen. As for reporting it, however, that could be a different story. If he left it out, one little detail, Padilla might have time to nose around and—

He was jarred out of his reverie by the insistent ringing of the telephone. He scowled and lifted the receiver on the second ring.

"Chavez."

"Captain Chavez?" It was a man's voice, speaking English.

"Yes. Who's this?"

"The name's Belasko, Captain. Is your line secure?"

"Excuse me?"

"We have business to discuss," the stranger said, "but it's for your ears only. If there's any chance that someone might be listening..."

Chavez glanced warily around the empty squad room, caught himself and said, "There's no one here."

"Well, if you're sure..."

Instinctively he thought about the switchboard. Might Padilla have arranged to have his phone calls monitored? Was he becoming paranoid?

"What is it that you wanted to discuss?"

"We need to talk about the Shining Path," the caller said. "And Garrick Hastings."

"If you have some information—"

"Face-to-face, I mean."

"Of course. My door is always open."

"I was thinking more of neutral ground."

"That is most irregular."

"You'll want to check me out, of course. I understand. Call Raymond Neary, at the U.S. Embassy. Are you familiar with the name?"

"I think so."

Neary was a "cultural attaché" at the embassy, well-known as an employee of the CIA. Chavez had met him several times, while sharing information on the Shining Path.

"Don't be afraid to wake him up," the stranger said. "Mention my name and ask him for the scoop."

"Belasko, was it?"

"Mike Belasko, right. I'll call you back in half an hour."

The line went dead, and Chavez dropped the handset back into its cradle. Suddenly his thoughts were racing. Did the stranger's call have anything to do with the events on Avenida Costanera? Could it be a mere coincidence, at that time of the morning, when most "public servants" were asleep?

No matter. He had to concentrate on first things first.

He was about to wake a chief of station for the CIA.

MERCY HASTINGS PACED around her hotel room, between the window and the bed, returning always to the street scene down below. She watched pedestrians in motion, heading off to early-morning jobs, and chafed at being grounded, waiting for a total stranger to call back and tell her what to do.

Three hours. He had used up forty minutes, as it was, and she wasn't about to wait one minute past the deadline. If he hadn't called by half past seven…then what?

If she backed off for a moment and was honest with herself, she knew that she was out of leads. It had been luck, as much as any skill on her part, that had put her onto Pirro Lopez. If a drunken would-be Romeo in one of the cantinas hadn't tried to awe her with his knowledge of the city's seamy side, she would be groping in the dark right now.

But it had been so easy, getting next to Lopez once she knew his name and where to find him on a given night. She wasn't the sort to brag about her looks, especially when she spent most of her time in OD uniforms, but neither was she blind. In truth, she knew how good she looked, and the effect she had on men, when she was trying. Sometimes even when she wasn't.

Lopez had been easy, if repulsive, and she was convinced he would have told her where his cronies had stashed her father, if Belasko hadn't interrupted her.

Goddammit!

Even in her anger and frustration, Hastings knew she couldn't blame Belasko for the screwup. Someone in the government had sent him to find her father, if she could believe his story, and he had no way of knowing she was on the case, much less that he would find her with a knife to Lopez's throat, in bed.

It made her blush to think of that part now, not Lopez— that was strictly business—but the way she had to have looked to this tall stranger who had dropped into the middle of her life. What could he think of her?

What did it matter?

Hastings thought about Belasko, thinking that his name had to be some kind of alias for starters, wondering why she should give a damn for his opinion. If he thought she was a shameless hussy or a stupid amateur, so what?

He was a pro, however; that was obvious. Three kills without a second thought, no wasted rounds, no hesitation. And it didn't seem to faze him afterward. The closest she had ever come to killing someone had been Lopez, straddling his chest and threatening to cut his head off if he didn't talk. Hastings believed she could have killed him, for her father's sake, to vent the rage and loathing Lopez had provoked. She had been trained to kill, but the training was all theoretical. The Army hadn't fired a shot in anger, anywhere, since she enlisted three years earlier, and Hastings knew the chances were that she could spend her twenty waiting for a war. She hadn't joined in hopes of killing, anyway; the notion had been service to her country, driven by a need to get out on her own, prove something to her father...and herself.

How much of that had driven her to seek him out, despite the risk of landing in a military jail, or even getting killed? She had no ready answer for that question, and it troubled her...but not enough to send her slinking back to Benning.

From what she had seen of the tall stranger in action, he would be a definite asset in the search for her father, not to mention any rescue effort that involved a clash with well-armed members of the Shining Path. She made a mental note to find a gun as soon as possible. They were available in Lima, she knew, but foreigners were at the bottom of the list in terms of favored customers with those who dealt in arms outside the law. Still, if she had to face another enemy—or even if it came down to a face-off with Belasko—she would need more than a five-inch dagger.

Part of her brain urged her to relax.

She recognized the wisdom of that advice, but it was difficult to put her emotions on hold. There was fear of losing her father, coupled with rage at his treatment by strangers, pent-up anger at the way she had been ordered to ignore the problem, mind her manners, toe the line.

Not this time.

She checked her watch again, saw that Belasko had two hours and fifteen minutes left. Still pacing, Hastings had her mind made up that she would move without him if he didn't call on time.

But part of her was hoping that he would, acknowledging the need for help. And if the help wasn't available...

"Hold on. I'm coming, Dad," she said aloud.

MIGUEL CARDOZA RECKONED he was running out of time. The sun had risen without Pirro Lopez answering his telephone, and it was stretching credibility to think that he was talking all this time. It had to be off the hook or out of order, to prevent Cardoza from getting through.

Dawn drove him from the service station, knowing as he did that the employees would be coming soon. It would go badly for him if they found him loitering around the place and called police. He had the pistol in his belt, but it would be a self-defeating gesture to engage in any kind of violent altercation with the pigs in daylight hours, when they could quickly summon reinforcements, track him down and put him in a cage, assuming he survived.

Cardoza still had work to do. He couldn't rest until someone from the Shining Path leadership heard his story of the raid on Avenida Costanera. If nothing else, he had to tell the story to protect himself against belated charges—cowardice, dereliction of duty, whatever—that might accrue because he had survived the raid.

Cardoza walked without direction, winding through the streets and trying not to be conspicuous. He knew where Pirro Lopez lived, and knew also that he couldn't show up there uninvited. Calling on the telephone was one thing, even that a grave breach of security, but in the circumstances, he didn't believe that Lopez would chastise him. At the moment his foremost concern was wasting so much time that someone else briefed Lopez on the raid and stirred up doubts about why Cardoza wasn't found among the dead.

The secrecy of the security police could help him there, he thought. They were notorious for freezing out the press on things like this, denying violent actions and suppressing evidence, sometimes presenting perjured testimony to the media and in the courts. It could be days before Lopez knew what had happened to his men, beyond the fact that they were dead and gone.

Cardoza still had a chance to get there with the inside story, if he did it soon enough, and he would simply have to pray that Lopez didn't kill the messenger.

Some of the shops were opening for business now, which made it that much easier for him to find a public telephone, but he couldn't spill out his tale with strangers listening. It would be necessary to arrange a meeting, have somebody pick him up and take him to a place where he could speak to Lopez privately.

Cardoza loitered at the window of a pastry shop, pretending interest in the sweets, eyes focused on the telephone inside. A small bell jangled overhead as he pushed through the doorway, and a smiling young woman came from somewhere in the back. He looked sheepish, nodding toward the telephone, but she didn't appear to mind. There were no other customers as he approached the telephone and dropped his coins into the slot, tapping out the number for perhaps the thirtieth time.

That time it rang. He could feel a sudden tightness in his throat and swallowed hard to clear the blockage. He didn't intend to stutter when he finally got through to Lopez.

"Hello."

He didn't recognize the voice, but assumed that it had to be one of Lopez's bodyguards. Still, there was something in the tone that stopped him from announcing his identity.

"Who's this?" he asked.

"Sergeant Batista, of security police. And who are *you?*"

Cardoza hung up the telephone before they had a chance to trace the call. Security police, at Lopez's home! What could it mean? Was the attack on Avenida Costanera part of some much larger drive against the Shining Path? Had the authorities finally cut through the layers of secrecy surrounding the organization? They had their tricks, of course, but that would almost have to mean a traitor in the ranks.

But who?

A sudden chill ran down Cardoza's spine. Suppose the brass got wind of what was happening, and somehow found out he was still alive before he had a chance to plead his case? Might they assume that he had cut a deal with the security police, sold out his comrades at the old apartment building—and Pirro Lopez, too—to save himself?

If *that* thought started taking hold with his superiors, Miguel Cardoza was as good as dead. His friends, and soldiers he had never seen, would be unleashed to shoot him down on sight. As long as he remained within the borders of Peru, he would be forced to live in hiding, like a hunted animal.

He left the pastry shop, resisting an impulse to grab one of the wrought-iron chairs and smash the glass display case in his rage. That it should come to this, when he had worked so hard and been so dedicated to the movement, risked his life so many times, it was a shameful travesty.

Still, he could save himself, if he was able to make contact with some other ranking officer and tell his tale persuasively. There was a chance. He still had hope.

Who would it be?

He searched his mind while walking down the sidewalk, almost perfectly oblivious to those around him. Instinct and long training made him watch out for police cars; otherwise, Cardoza might not have noticed if the sky was falling.

There was only one man higher in the movement than Lopez. Cardoza had never met the leader of the Shining Path—not *this* leader, who had taken over after Abimael Guzman Reynoso was arrested in 1992. He knew the leader's name, of course, and there were ways of reaching out to members of his staff, a number saved for dire emergencies, in case the standard chain of command was disrupted.

That was it. He had no other choice.

He would be forced to seek Alonzo Aguillar.

5

Captain Chavez was nervous as he motored south on Paseo de la Republica, watching his rearview mirror and praying that he wouldn't see another unmarked squad car tailing him. It was a short drive from the Palace of Justice to Neptune Park, close enough, perhaps, for a discreet tail to pursue him without being seen. Once he had reached the park, he could be tracked by sight, by directional microphones, any number of ways.

He *was* becoming paranoid, Chavez decided. Other than the voiced suspicions of the stranger he was on his way to meet, he had no reason to believe his office telephone was tapped or that his calls were being monitored in any way. Of course, Major Padilla and a number of his cronies had the power to do such things, but there was nothing to suggest that they had done so. As for Mike Belasko, on the other hand…

A sleepy Raymond Neary had come wide-awake when Chavez spoke the stranger's name. When he endorsed the stranger, it reminded Chavez of a would-be actor reading from a script, but what did that prove? Covers, codes and secrecy were everything in the intelligence community. Chavez saw quite enough of that himself, in his position with Peru's security police—the passion for control, for anonymity. And when Belasko called him back, precisely twenty-seven minutes later, Chavez had agreed to meet him in the sprawl of Neptune Park.

The captain parked his car and remained behind the wheel for several moments, making sure no other cars pulled in behind him. Finally satisfied, he left the vehicle, locked it and moved into the park itself. He smelled the grass and flowers, listened to a soft breeze rustling the leaves of trees and thought the park would be a peaceful place to die.

That morbid turn of thought had grown increasingly common with Chavez over the past year or so. The blood feud of the Shining Path had heated up in 1995, after the state proclaimed an amnesty for all police and soldiers charged, convicted or suspected of committing crimes against humanity. Chavez had personally viewed the action as a grave mistake, but he wasn't about to say so in the company of other officers. Since then, attacks upon the army and security police had increased nearly forty-five percent; some of Chavez's friends, most of them decent men, had paid the price for patting murderers and vicious bullies on the head, as if their crimes were tantamount to spitting on the sidewalk. Every morning, as he dressed for work, the captain was conscious of the fact that he could die that day, and no one in the world would grieve for him—except perhaps his cats.

No password or clandestine recognition signal had been specified, but Chavez knew Belasko at a glance. The tall American seemed perfectly at ease, but he didn't belong: too tall, too muscular, too—

Chavez caught himself. He recognized the face and felt his stomach twisting into knots. Was this a trap? His sport coat was unbuttoned, and he hooked a thumb inside his belt, to facilitate a fast draw of the pistol holstered under his left arm.

"Captain Chavez." There was no question in the stranger's voice.

"I know you."

"We've met, it's true," Bolan stated, "but we weren't introduced."

"So, it was you."

"Depends on what you mean."

"On Avenida Costanera," Chavez said. "You fought the Shining Path, and ran when the police arrived."

"So far, so good."

"You caused me personal embarrassment."

"I could have killed you," Bolan stated, "but I don't play that."

"Pardon?"

"I don't shoot cops."

"How civil of you." Chavez took a breath and held it, waiting for the anger to recede.

At length he asked, "What brings you to my city?"

"What you saw last night. I'm trying to retrieve a hostage."

"The American." This time it was Chavez who spoke with certainty.

"That's right. My people are convinced the Shining Path won't let him go, no matter what, and since our own stance on appeasing terrorists prevents us from requesting that you grant the group's demands..."

He left the rest of it unspoken.

"We have a law against assassination," Chavez told him.

"Depends on who you ask."

"I've never murdered anyone." Chavez could feel the warm flush rising in his face again.

"That's what I hear," Bolan said. "I need somebody I can trust."

"For what?" Chavez was openly suspicious now. This could turn out to be some kind of trick, a trap designed to catch him in some violation of the law. He wouldn't be surprised, in fact, to learn that Raymond Neary and the

CIA supported officers like Serafin Padilla, who saw Communists in every village where the peasants didn't kneel and kiss his boots.

"The hostage has a daughter," Bolan said. "She's in Lima, looking for a chance to help her father out."

"That's foolishness."

"I agree. We met when I dropped in to have a chat with Pirro Lopez earlier this morning. She was there ahead of me."

"Lopez? What happened?"

"You can pull your warrants, Captain. Pirro won't be building any more car bombs or sniping soldiers on the street."

"He's dead?"

"If not, I need to meet his personal physician," Bolan replied.

"He was murdered by the woman?"

"Did I say that?"

"Ah. You killed him."

"It was him or me. I didn't have to think about it very long."

"He won't be missed," Chavez admitted. "Still…" He put the thought on hold and asked, "What do you want from me?"

"A little help to keep the lady occupied," Bolan said. "She's AWOL from an Army unit in the States. If you could place her in protective custody and make some calls before you put her on a northbound flight, the MPs ought to keep her busy for a while."

"And leave you free to seek her father, yes?"

"Somebody has to try."

"What else?" Chavez was still suspicious, waiting for the other shoe to drop. "There must be something more."

"You mean, like asking you to give me a free hand?" Bolan smiled and shook his head. "Don't sweat it. Take care of the lady, and I'll owe you one. The payoff could be sweet."

Chavez stared into the American's eyes and knew he wasn't offering a bribe. The payoff he referred to would be something else, perhaps a chance for Chavez to strike hard against the Shining Path and boost his reputation in the process, maybe get Padilla off his back for good.

"Where can I find this woman?"

"For the next two hours, she'll be waiting at the Hotel Obregon, on Avenida Uruguay. Beyond that time, your guess would be as good as mine."

"I'll see to it myself," the captain said. "As for the rest of it..."

"Do what you have to do. Maybe I'll see you at the other end."

With that, he turned and walked away. Constantion Chavez stood watching him for several moments, then glanced sharply at his watch and started back in the direction of his waiting car.

EACH MORNING, when he woke to see another day, Alonzo Aguillar knew that he was a lucky man. He had slipped through the net, when the security police took Guzman and the others, back in 1993, and he had won the power struggle for control of the Shining Path, casting opposition to his leadership as treason to the cause. The fact that he was still alive, and still at liberty, confirmed the verdict of the palm reader in Comas who had told him that his life was charmed.

Which didn't mean he was immune to setbacks. At the moment, sitting in a warehouse on the bleak Chorillos waterfront, Aguillar had cause to wonder if his luck was running out. The previous night, one raid in Lima had annihilated close to twenty of his soldiers, while a separate incident had claimed the lives of Pirro Lopez and his bodyguards. It was impossible for Aguillar to view the incidents as unrelated, even though his eyes and ears in Lima told him Pirro had been murdered during sex, his watchdogs executed while going to his aid.

That much was no surprise. He had warned Lopez, more than once, that his sexual appetite was his own worst enemy, that it would get him killed someday. He could believe a woman killing Lopez, even gunning down his bodyguards if they were taken by surprise. Aguillar had a few female assassins in his group, and there were times when they had definite advantages...as with a man like Lopez, who did too much of his thinking with his cock.

All that was possible, but none of it explained *why* Lopez had been killed or how his death was linked to the preceding massacre. If the police had tracked him down, they would have sent a hundred uniforms to cage or kill Aguillar's second-in-command.

What then?

The answer—or one version of it—sat in front of him, perspiring freely, fidgeting beneath Aguillar's steady gaze. Miguel Cardoza had reached out to him through channels, more or less, upon discovering that Pirro Lopez had been killed. His story of the raid on Avenida Costanera had some most peculiar elements about it. The lone gunman, working downward from the top floor of the old apartment building with automatic weapons and grenades, dispatching roughly half of Cardoza's team before police arrived and he turned tail; Cardoza giving chase, but losing him in the confusion, doubling back to help his men, thus finding that he was cut off from the apartment building, no hope of breaking through the police line alive.

Aguillar had his doubts about this soldier's heroism, staring at him now, his nervous mannerisms echoing deception. Still, if he was lying, Aguillar suspected it was mostly in regard to his pursuit of the lone stranger who had launched the raid. It made no sense for him to fabricate a black-clad superman, if he had simply run away from the police. It would have been much easier for him to say that he had stepped out for a hot meal or a piece of ass, and then returned to find the neighborhood surrounded by police.

"This man in black," Aguillar said, "you didn't have a clear view of his face?"

"No, sir. The first time that I saw him, he was firing down the stairwell with a submachine gun, then he threw a hand grenade."

"It seems that luck was with you."

"Yes." Cardoza licked his lips. "Then, when I started chasing him, I only saw his back."

"I'm still not clear on how you lost him."

"When I got up to the roof," Cardoza said, "there was no sign of him. I knew he must go east or west, and westward was away from the police. I looked for him in that direction, but he must have gone the other way...or else he found a hiding place I didn't see."

"It's most unfortunate. You say he was a tall man?"

"Six feet, at the very least," Cardoza replied emphatically.

"And strong?"

"He seemed so. It's not easy to describe his clothes, some kind of black, tight-fitting garments, with a military harness over all. He had an athlete's body."

"Or a soldier's?"

"Perhaps."

"Could you identify this stranger if the two of you should meet again?"

Cardoza blinked and frowned at that. "I might," he said, then shook his head. "It would be difficult, Chief."

"Ah, well." Aguillar slipped a hand inside his jacket, reaching for his pistol. "Never mind."

He drew and fired in one smooth motion, seeing his bullet strike Cardoza above one eye. The second shot was better, the projectile boring in between Cardoza's open lips, to cut his spinal cord and exit from the rear in crimson mist.

"Dispose of that," Aguillar told the soldiers who were standing by. "It doesn't matter where."

Aguillar's driver fell in step beside him as he left the warehouse, walking to his car. His men would do as they were told, and no one in the Shining Path would miss Miguel Cardoza once the word got out that he had left his men to die while he ran off to save himself. A traitor made a fine example, every now and then.

Alonzo Aguillar had more-important problems to contend with at the moment. He was looking for a homicidal woman and a soldier dressed in black. If one of them found him before he tracked them down, it could be most unfortunate.

He stopped his driver halfway to the car and jerked his head in the direction of the warehouse, dark and silent now.

"Go back and tell the others that we're going to the country for a while," he said. "I need some breathing room."

"YOU'VE GOT AN HOUR, big boy."

Mercy Hastings sipped a can of soda, talking to herself. If that was evidence of craziness, so be it. When the smoke cleared, if she was alive, it wouldn't hurt to have a nice insanity defense on tap.

An hour remained until Belasko's deadline, but it troubled her that he hadn't called back already. What if something had gone wrong? He could be dead, and she would never know it, sitting in her hotel room and counting flyspecks on the wallpaper. And then again, he could be stalling her to get a head start on the manhunt for her father, making sure that she was sidelined while he did the work.

She knew a part of her would be relieved if that was true, if someone else could save her father's life and spare her from the need to kill anyone or crawl into bed with someone like that bastard Lopez. It was the thought of being handled and manipulated, like a child, that really set her teeth on edge. She was already facing brig time, with a possible bad-conduct discharge for the fact that she was AWOL. She had come this far, risked so much, that it was unthinkable to have a stranger trick her now, cheat her out of any opportunity to help her only living relative.

If Belasko found her father and retrieved him safely, that was one thing. If he failed, however, even got her father killed, perhaps, while she was sitting on her hands, well, Hastings didn't know if she could live with that.

She should be out there, looking for her father, instead of killing time and waiting for a man she barely knew to call and give her his permission to proceed. Who was he, anyway? She didn't buy the CIA connection—maybe in the old days, back before congress started butting into things, but not today—and yet she couldn't think of any other agency that might be likely to attempt a mission of this sort.

It was a mystery, and what she needed at the moment was an answer, not more questions to confuse her quest.

"I'm getting out of here," she told the walls, and scooped up her bag from the dresser, checking to make sure her money, passport and the dagger were inside. The first thing she would have to do was find herself a gun, against the prospect of some heavy action down the line. From there...

She closed the door behind her, heard the automatic lock click into place and was turning toward the elevators when she saw the uniforms, three officers from the security police, together with a suit who seemed to be in charge. The four men saw her as she spotted them, and Hastings heard the suit say something, though she couldn't catch the words.

She started reaching for her key, then stopped herself. The room would only be a trap, assuming she could even get the door unlocked before they tackled her. The uniforms were closing in as Hastings bolted, running in the opposite direction, heading for the service stairs.

How had they known where she was staying? Why would they be looking for her in the first place, unless—

Mike Belasko!

He had sold her out, the bastard. Whether he believed she would be better off in custody or if he simply didn't give a damn, it all worked out the same. She had a score to settle with the man once she shook these characters.

Assuming she could shake them.

Mercy Hastings was a soldier and an athlete, built for speed. She had exchanged her high heels for a pair of running shoes, her slinky dress for shirt and jeans. She did her best, and almost made it.

Almost.

Something struck the back of her legs, below the knees, and slid between them, tripping her. She threw her hands out, falling heavily, sustaining carpet burns on both her open palms. A backward glance showed her the nightstick one of her assailants had to have thrown to bring her down.

She scrambled to her feet, one hand inside her bag and groping for the knife, but then they were on top of her, had pinned her arms and snatched the purse away. She kicked one in the shin, and found herself against the wall, breasts flattened by the weight of someone leaning on her back, an elbow gouging her between the shoulder blades.

Her arms were twisted painfully behind her back. She clenched her teeth and waited for another chance to break away.

"It seems we must use handcuffs," someone said in Spanish. Hastings knew it had to be the suit. "But gently, please," he added. "This one is a friend. She simply doesn't know it yet."

HIS ENEMIES WERE on their guard by now, and striking in the daylight hours carried special risks, but Bolan had a list of targets waiting to be razed or rattled. There was no time like the present to continue with his blitz, now that the Mercy Hastings problem had been solved, and Bolan knew that every moment wasted was an opportunity that he would never have again.

Suburban San Martin de Porras lies just over a mile west of downtown Lima, and roughly one-half mile east of the airport. Its main drag, and dividing line between industrial and residential neighborhoods, is Avenida Peru, running east-west through the very heart of town. A left turn, one block east brought Bolan to a district where light industry and aging warehouses lined streets devoid of children. Bolan found his target halfway down the block and on his left, ostensibly a small machine shop, where the Shining Path stockpiled, modified and manufactured military hardware.

Bolan parked behind a warehouse that was up for lease. He checked the Uzi's load and screwed on the suppressor, fastening the weapon to a swivel harness worn beneath his windbreaker. The day hadn't begun to heat up, and Bolan's lightweight jacket wouldn't make him too conspicuous, assuming there was anyone to see him in the hundred yards before he reached his goal.

He came at the machine shop from behind and found two aging vans backed up against the wall on either side

of the rear exit. Both vehicles had their side doors open,
waiting for some kind of cargo to be shuttled in or out.
Would they be loading or unloading here?

He had his answer seconds later, when a young man
exited the stucco building, bent beneath the weight of
something in a giant duffel bag. He rolled the bag into
the nearer van, and Bolan heard its weighty contents clank
like metals tools.

Or guns.

From all appearances, some kind of major move was
under way, and the Executioner had arrived in time to
interrupt the bailout. It was clearly not a one-man job, this
brisk evacuation, and he had no way of counting heads
from where he stood. That would have to wait until he
was inside the shop.

He waited for another young man to carry one more
bulging, clanking load of arms—into the other van, this
time—before he made his move. It was no more than
thirty feet from where he stood to reach the nearer van,
and Bolan had his Uzi clear before he got there, thumbing
off the safety, edging in between the vans to face the
shop's back door.

He kept on going and made it almost to the doorstep
unobserved. Then the first young terrorist came back with
yet another load, two heavy toolboxes this time, one in
either hand. The shooter had a pistol in his belt, but there
was no way he could reach it, draw and fire in time to
save himself. He tried it anyway, releasing one of the
heavy boxes with his right hand and reaching for the gun,
the toolbox on his left immediately throwing him off
balance.

Bolan shot him in the chest, a muffled 3-round burst
that slammed his target backward, took him down, the
second toolbox banging hard and loud against the concrete floor. That finished any hope of sneaking up on those

inside. The Executioner rushed the doorway and charged across the threshold, with a little hop to clear the supine body of his fallen enemy.

Inside, the shop was basically a one-room operation, with a standing lathe, drill press and other tools arranged haphazardly around a space that measured roughly twenty by fifteen. There was a large hydraulic lift, dead center in the room, in case they had to work on cars. It was elevated now, some six or seven feet above the floor. A man was peering from the pit and watching Bolan, frozen with his hands braced on the OD duffel bag that he had lately hoisted up and out. Two other soldiers had been frozen by his entrance, one down on his knees beside an open toolbox, while the other stood with shoulders hunched beneath the weight of yet another loaded duffel bag.

They had enough guns there to arm an infantry battalion, but the only ones that mattered, at the moment, were the pistols in their belts. The kneeling man was quickest off the mark, crab-walking toward the pit and hauling out a shiny autoloader, swinging it into a firm two-handed grip.

The move was almost good enough, but Bolan hit him with a rising burst that turned his crouch into a jerky little break-dance, leaving him crumpled on the floor while crimson pooled beneath his body.

Off to Bolan's left, the standing gunner dropped his duffel, but the thick strap snagged his gun arm in the process, slowing him, and he was nowhere close to clearing leather when a spray of parabellum rounds tore through him, lifting him completely off his feet and slamming him against a wooden workbench, pinning him before he tumbled, boneless, to the floor.

And that left one.

The shooter in the pit got off a shot, but he was firing blind, his gun hand thrust above floor level, while the rest of him stayed out of sight. It was a disadvantage for him, but he could have other weapons down there, maybe even frag grenades.

Instead of taking chances, Bolan found the wall switch that controlled the lift, pure logic standing in for fluent Spanish as he started lowering the heavy metal framework. Down below, his adversary gave a frightened little squeal, but there were no words to it, nothing that would indicate surrender.

Bolan stopped the lift when it was several inches from the floor and moved in closer, careful not to make himself a target in the process. He stood by and gave the mole man time to think about his plight before he spoke.

"Do you speak English?"

"*Sí.*"

"So, prove it."

"I speak English," said the small voice from the pit.

"Okay. I've got a deal for you."

"*¿Quien es?* I mean, what is it?"

"I need information," Bolan said. "You give it to me, and I let you live."

"What information?" He sounded cautious now, despite the hopelessness of his predicament.

"I need to know where you were going with the guns."

"I don't know."

"Fine with me."

He walked back to the wall switch, brought the lift down another inch before his captive stopped him with a breathless cry.

"No, wait! I tell you."

Bolan crouched beside the pit and said, "I'm listening."

"There is a camp, a few miles north of Yauyos, in the jungle. Let me out, and I can take you there."

"I don't think so," the Executioner replied.

"I tell the truth," the cellar dweller said.

"I'm counting on it." Bolan rose and turned away.

"You promised to release me!"

"You need to get your hearing checked. I said I'd let you live."

Outside, the air smelled fresh, without the reek of cordite in his nostrils. Bolan tucked the Uzi out of sight and walked back to his car. A call to the police, if they weren't already on their way, would give the soldier in the pit some breathing room. However he responded to the sight of uniforms, with all those weapons handy, was entirely up to him.

The Executioner was moving on. He had a long drive still ahead of him before his next appointment with the enemy, and he didn't intend to keep them waiting any longer than was absolutely necessary.

He was on a roll.

The troops of the Shining Path could look forward to a taste of hell on earth.

6

Instead of clapping Mercy Hastings in a cell, her captors had proceeded to a safehouse—actually a two-bedroom apartment. Once inside the flat, they took the handcuffs off and returned her purse, with two items missing.

"I'm afraid the knife won't pass inspection at the airport," said Captain Chavez. "Your passport will be returned to you once you've cleared immigration and are safely on the plane."

"You can't just kick me out like this," she said. "I rate a hearing."

"That is true," the captain agreed, "if you insist upon your rights. In that case, there will be the weapons charge to deal with, plus the matter of assaulting a policeman and defying his authority. I have no doubt the U.S. Embassy can manage your release within a week or so. If trial is waived on the assorted criminal offenses, I believe you may find military escorts waiting to discuss a certain soldier who is missing from her post."

So, that was the deal, she thought, and shrugged it off. If there were any latent doubts about Belasko's role in her arrest, they vanished as the captain spoke, and she was left to brood in silence with a pair of stone-faced guards: one from the team that picked her up, the other a petite but rugged-looking female who was obviously summoned to avoid a beef for sexual harassment.

Hastings settled in the larger of the bedrooms, waiting,

with the door left open under orders from her watchdogs. Stretched out on the double bed, pretending to relax, she fumed and stared holes in the ceiling, willing her pulse to stabilize as she racked her brain for a way to escape.

And find Belasko. The bastard would regret betraying her. That much she promised to herself, whatever else she managed to accomplish for her father.

Payback was a bitch, she thought. And so was she.

It took some moments for her mind to register the conversation that her guards were having in the living room. They didn't bother whispering, most likely unaware that she spoke Spanish. Hastings lay and listened as they talked about a raid some officer with the security police was planning on a Shining Path encampment north of Yauyos.

Where in hell was that? Forget it—she could always get herself a map. Locating cities was the least of her problems at the moment. She would have to get out of the safehouse somehow, ditch her watchdogs and proceed from there.

Her brain went back to work. Safehouses, she considered, were primarily employed for subjects who were glad to be sequestered, hidden from some outside enemy. They were designed as prisons, since the normal fear was of someone breaking *in*, not sneaking *out*.

She checked the nearest window without rising from her bed. The curtains were open, and she saw that it was locked, but there were no bars on the window, nothing to prevent a person crawling in or out if the latch could be beaten. She couldn't use the bedroom window, though, because her female escort sat directly opposite the open door, where any movement Hastings made would capture her attention instantly. The pair of them would tackle her before she had a chance to scramble through the window; that was clear.

But if she found another window, where they couldn't see her...

There was only one way she could go, and if it failed, if they were ready for her somehow, she was screwed. One failed attempt to flee, and they would put the handcuffs back on, perhaps secure her to the bed, until Chavez came back to fetch her to the airport.

When was the next flight from Lima to the States? She didn't have a clue, but every minute wasted now put her that much closer to disgrace and failure. She wasn't concerned about the military charges she would face. If she could help her father, and it put her in the brig, it would be cheap at half the price. But if she failed, if no one got him back at all, she knew his death would haunt her for the rest of her miserable life.

She knew what had to be done and didn't hesitate, removing money from her purse and tucking it inside a pocket of her jeans. The female officer glanced over as she got up from the bed, a small frown on her face. As Hastings reached the bedroom doorway, both escorts were on their feet.

"I need to use the bathroom," she informed them.

They exchanged suspicious glances, but the female nodded, while her counterpart just shrugged and sat back down. Hastings proceeded to the bathroom, with the female cop behind her. On the threshold, she turned back to face her jailer.

"Did you want to watch," she asked, "or may I close the door?"

"Don't lock it."

"God forbid."

She closed the door behind her, looked for something she could jam beneath the knob, and came up empty. Never mind. She had a few spare minutes; she would have to use them well.

She moved directly to the window. It was set above the tap end of a smallish bathtub that hadn't been cleaned since God knew when. The glass was frosted, but Hastings saw no shadows on the outside that would indicate a set of mounted burglar bars. The window wasn't large, but with a little luck, she thought that she could wriggle through. The latch, while stiff from long disuse, began to move as she applied some force.

Okay.

She stepped back from the tub, walked over to the toilet, waiting half a minute more before she pulled some toilet tissue off the squeaky roll and dropped it into the commode. She pressed the handle, flushing it, and moved directly to the sink. Turning on both taps, she left them running as she went back to the tub, stepped in and used the short neck of the faucet as her next step up.

The window opened with a gritty scraping sound, but Hastings didn't hesitate. She gripped the sill and pushed off with her left foot, head and shoulders squeezing through the gap. She scraped her breasts and stomach painfully, but clenched her teeth and kept on pushing with both hands against rough stucco on the outside wall. For just a moment, she was worried that her hips might jam and trap her there, but with an extra grinding twist, she made it through. From that point, gravity took over, and she tumbled forward, headfirst toward the ground, some fifteen feet below. She just had time to execute a rough half somersault and slam down on her buttocks, wincing at the pain.

A second later she was up and running. Somewhere at her back and overhead, she heard the female cop begin to curse and shout in Spanish, ordering her sidekick to get off his ass and run downstairs.

Too late.

When Mercy Hastings hit the nearest side street, she

was on her way. She had to bag some wheels, first thing, and then a gun, a map, directions to this Yauyos place. It was a long shot, but it was the best lead she had. Her only chance was to lay hands on yet another member of the Shining Path and squeeze him until he spilled his guts.

But she wasn't forgetting Mike Belasko, either. Not in this life.

And if her father died because Belasko had delayed her search, there would be hell to pay.

THE TIP HAD COME IN from a forty-nine-year-old informant who was trying desperately to save her only living child. The peasant woman had already lost three sons to firing squads or skirmishes with soldiers, and her fourth—and last—had joined the Shining Path as soon as he was old enough, intending to avenge his brothers. For the past three years, he had been running guns, participating on the fringes of the movement. His mother didn't think that he had murdered anyone so far, but what did she know?

Major Serafin Padilla had received the tip from one of his subordinates, though he would certainly take credit for it when he wrote up his report. The woman had been talking to a corporal, who had told his sergeant, who alerted his lieutenant—so on, up the ladder of command. She wanted to exchange some information for a promise that her son wouldn't be harmed if he was captured by the army or security police.

Major Padilla gave his word without a second thought. What difference did it make? Let her complain, after the smoke cleared, that a troop of soldiers in a firefight should select by name which enemies they killed in self-defense.

Padilla wished her luck. Assuming that she was deranged enough by grief to make a public protest, she could always have an accident. Meanwhile the major had more pressing matters on his mind.

According to the peasant woman, soldiers of the Shining Path from Lima and environs had been summoned to a meeting north of Yauyos. There were rumors that Alonzo Aguillar himself would meet them, the first time in almost eighteen months that he had surfaced in a gathering of any size. Padilla meant to be there when it happened, with as many men and guns as possible.

Of course, the meeting site's location was a mystery, but it was fairly obvious that some point closer to the mountain town had been intended as the meeting place. Padilla was familiar with the area in general terms, but he would be employing local guides. If no one in the neighborhood knew anything about the meeting, he would find it on his own. And if they lied to him, attempted to deceive him, well, Padilla had his own time-honored methods for dealing with those who harbored terrorists.

The main thing now was keeping up security. He knew that word of the informant's story had already spread beyond his circle of subordinates. Padilla would have bet his life, however, that the details of his plan were known to no one but himself and the supreme commander of the security police. The men, weapons and vehicles had been assembled quietly, behind deliberate rumors of a training exercise. The troops selected for his mission would be told the truth when they were safely on their way, and not before. Padilla would allow no leaks to neighbors, friends or lovers that might somehow get back to the keen ears of the Shining Path.

He had them this time, Padilla thought. Aguillar, his chief lieutenants and a fair-sized group of rebel soldiers all collected in one place and waiting for the ax to fall. The major knew that he could wait long years and never see another opportunity like this one. He couldn't allow it to slip through his fingers, when the smell of victory was so strong in his nostrils.

Not this time.

The officer who crushed the Shining Path once and for all could claim whatever prize he wanted in Peru. A fling at politics would be the least of it, with all the grateful corporations, ranchers, manufacturers, investment houses—the possibilities were endless! Alonzo Aguillar's head on a stick was worth millions, and Padilla meant to be the one who cashed that winning ticket in.

He would be going with his soldiers this time, to make sure that everything was done correctly. On some less important raid, it would be fine for him to sit behind his desk in Lima, leaving the decisions to his field commander, but with so much riding on the line, Padilla didn't want to run the risk of letting anyone share in the glory.

Not when he could claim it for himself.

This victory would be all his, and if something went wrong, there would be lower-ranking officers on standby to accept the blame. It was the beauty of Padilla's job that no one of command rank was responsible for anything, unless he chose to be.

And Serafin Padilla wouldn't choose responsibility for the events he was about to set in motion unless there was profit in the outcome for himself.

He stood before a full-length mirror, checking out his battle dress, deciding he was ready. It was time to go. He had already kept the others waiting long enough.

This time tomorrow, he would be a hero in his native land, or else he would remain exactly as he was, no change at all. It was a win-win situation for Padilla, and it made him smile as he went out to meet his troops.

"WHAT DO YOU MEAN, she got away?"

It was a foolish question, Constantion Chavez thought

as soon as he had spoken, but the news required some kind of a response, and he could think of nothing else. The telephone receiver suddenly felt clammy in his hand, causing his grip to tighten, blanching color from his knuckles.

Chavez sat and listened while the sergeant, Hector Ramos, stammered out an explanation, trying not to make himself look like a total idiot. They had allowed their prisoner to use the bathroom at the safehouse, and she had escaped by climbing through the window. Simple, just like that. Her escorts were aware of the escape before she reached the nearest street, but shouting after her was useless, forcing Ramos to run back downstairs and chase her, while his smaller female partner tried the window route, for quicker access to the ground. It was a fluke that she had sprained her ankle on a short and relatively easy drop, Ramos said. As for him, the woman had already disappeared before he got downstairs. A one-man search was hopeless, and he knew that Captain Chavez had described the case as "sensitive." Accordingly no reinforcements had been summoned prior to Ramos checking with his boss.

Try as he might, Chavez could find no real fault with the sergeant's logic. It wasn't his fault that burglar bars had been considered too extravagant and obvious for mounting on the windows. No one ever thought about a suspect in protective custody escaping voluntarily. This was the first time a reluctant guest had tested the facility, and it had failed.

Chavez experienced a mingled sense of anger and relief. The latter feeling was occasioned by the fact that none of his superiors knew he had grabbed the daughter of a missing U.S. diplomat and locked her up against her will, for an illegal summary expulsion from the country. It wasn't the most outrageous act performed by any captain of the security police, but the suggestion of a clash with the United States over a woman would be bad enough, if it came out. As for Chavez cooperating with the tall American who called himself Belasko, well...

The captain was relieved to have that sticky problem snatched out of his hands and thrown back to the Fates. He had already sworn the several officers involved to secrecy, for what that might be worth, and he would never himself breathe a word of it to anyone. As for the woman, she was on her own. Chavez had done his part, but there was no way he could launch a major hunt in Lima without raising some high-ranking eyebrows in the process. Serafin Padilla would be thankful for the opportunity to bring him down, and there were others, too, who wouldn't mind if Chavez fell from grace.

As for his anger, it derived from failure on a mission that would have to rank among the easiest of his career. Pick up a woman, hold her for a few short hours and put her on an airplane. What was simpler than that? Chavez imagined he could do it in his sleep.

But something had gone wrong, and he had failed. It made no difference that one of his predecessors had approved the flat and recommended no improvements, or that he hadn't been present when the woman made her getaway. It galled him all the same, reflecting on his competence and his command. It shouldn't trouble him so much, that he had failed a total stranger on a mission that was neither his concern nor rightful duty, but the sense of failure dogged him all the same.

Belasko was supposed to call him back. "I'll owe you one," the tall American had said. "The payoff could be sweet." What would he say now, when Belasko asked about the woman? There would be no point in lying, when she could resurface anywhere, at any time. Chavez wasn't concerned about the American's payoff at the moment;

that was lost, in any case. But it would be a shame to him, admitting that he couldn't do the simplest thing, like keeping a defenseless woman under lock and key.

At least, he had her passport, Chavez thought before considering that it might be a further liability. The document linked him to her arrest—or her abduction, as a purist might suggest—and it could yet come back to haunt him. He considered burning it, but compromised by locking it inside his desk, where he believed it would be safe for the time being. If the woman never claimed it, he could always think about disposal later on.

He wondered where she was—more curiosity than any wish to drag her back—and whether she would keep on with the quest to find her father. She had nothing but the clothes upon her back, perhaps some cash. What could she do?

Unfortunately he already knew the answer to that question. She could poke her nose into the Shining Path's business and get killed. She could be lost without a trace, and who would ever know what happened to her then?

Chavez knew he should put the problem out of mind, but it wasn't that easy. He felt a responsibility to Mike Belasko, by extension to the woman. There was nothing he could do to help her, but Chavez knew that her death would haunt him, if and when it came.

And so, he thought, what else was new?

There were now enough ghosts on his conscience to fully occupy a fair-sized haunted house. Victims of terrorist attacks, whom he had been unable to protect; civilians brutalized or killed by members of his own department, in defiance of the law; their parents, siblings, widows, orphans. So much blood and misery.

He shrugged off the morbid feeling and turned back to the pile of thick manila folders stacked on his desk.

Chavez had work to do.

The rest of it would have to wait.

THE HELL OF IT was pushing off without a clear destination in mind. Bolan had run a hasty check through Stony Man, and his support team had come back with satellite surveillance photos of the Andes foothills north of Yauyos. There was too much cover for a clear look at the ground, which would have told him where the Shining Path guerrillas had their camp, but infrared photography had picked out two locations within ten or twelve miles to the north, where readings verified substantial human habitation.

He would have to check them both, and hope that one of them paid off. If both sites proved to be no more than native villages, he would be forced to try another angle of attack.

He would be screwed, in fact, with nothing left for him to do but start from scratch, in Lima, while his quarry went to ground who knew where.

It was too early yet for a defeatist attitude, and Bolan cleared his mind of negatives as he finished dressing for the jungle, cinching up his battle harness, double-checking weapons and support gear, dabbing war paint on his face and hands. The rental car was hidden to the best of his ability, well off a narrow, unpaved road that wound among the foothills a half mile north of Yauyos.

He would have to do the rest of it on foot.

He had coordinates for both potential targets, and would check the closer of them first. The satellite had been unable to predict how many people would be waiting for him there. More than forty but less than a hundred, the computer told him, with a margin of error pegged at plus or minus five percent.

Terrific.

That left him looking for a jungle hardsite boasting at

least thirty-eight guns, perhaps as many as one hundred and five. The uncertainty was worse than killer odds, to Bolan's way of thinking. He had faced tight odds before and walked away from it, but ignorance could get him killed.

His head weapon for the strike was a Steyr AUG assault rifle, the bullpup design that included a factory-standard muzzle launcher for MECAR 40 mm rifle grenades. For backup he was carrying the Uzi SMG with sound suppressor attached, and the Beretta 93-R selective-fire automatic was snug in its shoulder holster beneath his left arm. A Ka-bar fighting knife, spare magazines in canvas pouches, plus a fair assortment of grenades completed the ensemble.

He was dressed to kill and ready for the trail.

Yauyos is sixty-seven miles southeast of Lima, on the west slope of the Cordillera Occidental. At an altitude of five thousand feet above sea level, it made a long hike tiring, but it could have been much worse. Another fifty miles due east, the mighty Andes reared their jagged heads to twenty thousand feet and better.

The altitude was helpful, in a way. It lowered temperatures and kept the breeze refreshing, cut down on mosquitoes and assorted other stinging pests. He wouldn't sweat as much as someone hiking through the lowlands, even if it took a bit more oxygen to keep him going.

With a compass to direct him, he should make his first stop well before the sun went down. If he got lucky, hit the Shining Path encampment on his first attempt, then he would wait for dark and make his final plans for the attack. If not, then he would have another trek in front of him, continuing through darkness, until he was close enough to see, hear, smell the second settlement. If that site was a washout, he would have a long walk back, with nothing much to show for it. And while it wouldn't be the first letdown in the Executioner's years of endless war against the savages, he never took defeat as something to be shrugged away.

That grand old warhorse, General George S. Patton, once declared that he could never give a damn for any man who lost and laughed about it.

Bolan wasn't laughing now.

His eyes turned northward, found a narrow trail among the trees and he was on his way.

7

The idea came to Major Padilla on the slow drive south from Lima, down to Yauyos. There was no way to conceal a caravan of military vehicles, and simple logic told him that the Shining Path had eyes along their route. His enemies might very well be warned that he was coming, and there wasn't much—if anything—that he could do to stop the word from spreading.

Maybe he could minimize it, though, with a diversion that would keep the men he hunted looking elsewhere, watching in the wrong direction while he crept up on their blind side and destroyed them.

In the process, Padilla thought, he might even save himself to fight another day.

Since rolling out of Lima, he had started to consider all the risks that were involved in leading the attack himself. It was heroic, certainly—the kind of gesture that newspapers loved—and it would set a fine example for his men...but what if he got killed? The prospect made Padilla reconsider, thinking through his options, and he finally decided on a compromise that seemed to meet all of his needs at once. He would remain in Yauyos with a company of soldiers, sending out patrols in various directions as if he had no idea where the Shining Path had its camp. The northbound force would drag its heels until the teams dispatched to east and west had time to make a rendezvous. The larger, stronger team would then proceed as ordered and attempt to flush the enemy.

Because, in fact, Padilla did *not* know exactly where his enemies were located. His source had managed to supply the general location, but a search was still required by soldiers on the ground. Their first strike was to be directed at the village of Tristan del Sol.

The choice had been deliberate on Padilla's part. Tristan del Sol bred rebels; he was sure of it. The name cropped up on three or four arrest reports within the past year and a half, a figure that surprised Padilla when he weighed the hundreds of arrests made by security police each month against the ninety-odd inhabitants who occupied Tristan del Sol. Clearly the peasants had been up to no good in their village. Now, with confirmation that the Shining Path maintained a base camp in the area, Padilla thought he knew the reason why.

The village had been searched before, without result, and he wasn't about to waste his time in one more futile round of poking into peasant hovels, looking for a stray gun here and there. It was enough for him to know the villagers had rebel sympathies. For that, they would be punished, used as an example for their neighbors.

They would have to die.

Padilla could have used the death squads, but he needed an official presence in the area for when he flushed the Shining Path guerrillas from their hideaway. The razing of Tristan del Sol would be explained away as part of the campaign against Alonzo Aguillar. If necessary, weapons could be planted in the village to confirm the link between its residents and the subversives he intended to destroy.

Besides, he asked himself, who would be concerned about the death of a few peasants when there was a major victory against the Shining Path to celebrate? Padilla could expect a medal for his efforts, at the very least.

Promotion was possible. What limits were there for a hero, with his name on everybody's lips?

And he could do it all in safety, with a minimal exposure to the risks of combat. Let his soldiers spot the enemy, engage him, corner him and make the kill. Padilla was the officer in charge, and he would be there when it counted: when the cameras started snapping pictures for posterity. It would be *his* report the brass reviewed and rubber-stamped, unanimous approval for a job well done. There would be no dissenting witnesses to contradict Padilla's version of events. Not in his own ranks, and certainly not on the other side.

Padilla wasn't taking any prisoners this time. If that seemed strange, perhaps suspicious, he could readily explain the rebel death toll as a product of their own fanaticism. So committed were they to destruction of the state, that they wouldn't surrender, even in the face of overwhelming odds. If certain peasants thought that made them martyrs, dying like the zealots at Masada, well, there would be time enough to educate such fools at leisure, once Padilla finished looking out for number one.

The mayor of Yauyos greeted him with something less than absolute enthusiasm, but Padilla didn't take offense. He understood these local politicians, large frogs in their tiny ponds, both jealous and suspicious of the world outside. When that world barged into their lives, they tried to make the best of it, without surrendering their own positions in the process.

Certainly, the mayor informed Padilla, he was happy to cooperate in putting down a plot against the state. It would be no great imposition to supply the major's men with temporary quarters while their comrades were patrolling in the forest. If the troops required an extra generator, one could almost certainly be found.

The mayor wanted no trouble from Padilla. He would

play along and pretend that most of it had been his own idea. Before the day was out, he might convince himself.

Now all Padilla had to do was sit and wait for the reports of victory to reach his ears. Tristan del Sol would be the first. And afterward...

The big one.

He could afford to wait.

The major knew that time was on his side.

WITH LIMITED RESERVES of cash, Mercy Hastings decided she should steal a car instead of renting one. Besides, the rental office would require ID, and she had none remaining, since the captain took her passport and she left her purse behind while fleeing her "protectors."

The theft was no great problem, in itself. Hastings had learned to hot-wire cars in high school and refreshed her skills on an assignment to the motor pool, her first year in the service. As it happened, though, she found a compact with the keys in the ignition, parked outside a smallish shopping center on Jiron Oroya. By the time its owner left the nearby pastry shop, his ride was gone and she was in the wind.

The gun wasn't as simple. The laws restricting ownership of firearms in Peru dated back to the days of military rule. They were routinely flaunted by a certain class of natives, but a foreigner couldn't flash money in a sporting-goods emporium and walk out with a weapon in a shopping bag. She had to ask five taxi drivers in a row before she found one who would help her out, the risk increasing every time one frowned and shook his head. She was about to give it up, when number five agreed to help her, introducing Hastings to a pawnshop owner who, in turn, suggested that it might be possible for her to buy a weapon if she had sufficient cash in hand.

The dealer's pistols were his most expensive items, and

least suitable for what she had in mind. She wound up settling for a vintage 12-gauge pump gun, with a pistol grip and shortened barrel. Broken down, it fit conveniently into a leather gym bag, which she also purchased from the dealer, along with two hundred rounds of double-aught buckshot. The total package cost roughly twice what Mercy would have paid for similar equipment in the States, but she was in a seller's market and she had no time to shop around.

She had the cabbie drop her off a block from where her stolen car was parked, providing him with no opportunity to make another killing by reporting her to the police, complete with license numbers for an easy bust. As for the pawnshop owner, he wasn't in a position to betray her, even if he knew her name, which he didn't. She still had cash enough to fill the car with gas and buy some junk food for the road.

Speaking of roads, they were the worst. A few miles out of Lima, pavement gave way to concrete, poorly maintained, and that in turn gave way to gravel over dirt as she increased her distance from the city. Hastings knew that she was losing time, but it wouldn't be any benefit if she sped up and cracked the oil pan, maybe broke an axle in her haste. On foot, she might as well give up.

If there was any consolation, she found it in the fervent hope that Mike Belasko might be back in Lima, side-tracked with his business of harassing the Shining Path while she put more ground between them, chasing down the one lead that might help her find her father.

Just about the time the pavement ended, though, she started having doubts—none serious enough to make her turn around—she had no other leads, in any case—but still disturbing. What if the reports of Shining Path activity near Yauyos were mistaken, or worse yet, completely unrelated to her father's kidnapping? She could be driving head-on toward collision with a hornet's nest, while some distinct and separate team of terrorists was covering her father, miles and miles away.

She was running with the only hope she had, and if it failed her, then at least she could look back and know that she had done her best. It made no sense to her that they would keep him anywhere in Lima, when the town was crawling with security police on full alert, and there was nowhere else for her to go.

If all else failed, she could try to grab another rebel, make him talk, with no more interruptions this time.

And when she got to Yauyos, then what would she do? Shotgun aside, Hastings had nothing in the way of usual equipment for a jungle trek: no boots or camouflage fatigues; no pack, provisions, canteen, drinking water, maps or compass, knife or matches—not a goddamned thing, in fact.

She dragged out the glove compartment's contents and found a plastic flashlight that appeared to work, though she could hardly judge its strength in daylight. Registration papers. One street map for Lima. Half a dozen crumpled paper napkins.

"Shit!"

She would be forced to stop in Yauyos and attempt to buy some gear, without attracting much attention to herself. Her jeans and shirt would serve as clothing on the trail if she could do no better. Likewise with her running shoes, if she could find no decent hiking boots. As for the rest of it, the best that she could do was keep her fingers crossed and hope.

The seeming hopelessness of her endeavor struck her then, and the woman almost turned the car around. Almost. Iron will alone kept her from heading back to Lima. She had come this far, and there was nothing in the city for her but defeat. If she drove on to Yauyos, made her trek into the jungle and she still couldn't locate her father, at least Hastings would have done her best.

CAPTAIN VIRGILIO Menendez watched his pointmen, who were at the limit of his vision in that gloomy forest, and couldn't help wondering if they were walking into trouble. He had gone that route before, and while it didn't frighten him, he had the combat veteran's classic interest in surviving so that he could fight again another day.

At least this time he didn't have to hide his face.

Their mission was straightforward, perfectly legitimate, although he acknowledged that some civilians would be getting hurt along the way. That risk was part of every war, and any soldier who couldn't accommodate the fact didn't belong in uniform.

As for the men who found it *easier* to kill unarmed civilians than a normal enemy, well, there were other avenues for them, as well.

Menendez had pursued both angles of attack in recent years. He was a chief liaison officer between his field commander, Major Serafin Padilla, and a paramilitary death squad that included former cops and soldiers, most of them cashiered from service over accusations of brutality or wrongful death. It made no difference to the liberals that such men were devoted patriots, prepared to go the limit for their country, even at the risk of prison or untimely death before a firing squad.

Of course, the threat of being brought to trial was lessening these days, what with the amnesty for any officer convicted or accused of human-rights abuses. *That* had made the liberals and communists go crazy, bitching to the impotent United Nations as if that collection of pathetic sycophants could understand, much less control, events transpiring in Peru.

It was a kind of fluke that brought Menendez into con-

tact with the covert-action squads. A number of his col-
leagues had been pressured to resign for beating information out of terrorists, a few of whom had subsequently
died, and when the leftist inquisition somehow missed
Menendez, they were overjoyed. A phone call and a string
of late-night meetings did the rest. Menendez took the
plan upstairs, aware before he ever spoke to Padilla that
the major sympathized wholeheartedly with the position
of his comrades.

So the deal was struck to keep a "special squad" on
tap for situations when the rules of the security police
forbade Padilla and his men in uniform from dealing with
specific problems in specific ways. A terrorist who wriggled out of prison on a technicality, or who escaped in-
dictment altogether, could expect a visit from the *other*
men who stood for law and order in Peru. Whole families
had been known to disappear—and once, at least, a whole
rebellious village—and the system worked.

So far.

This raid was different, on several counts. Their target
was legitimate, for one thing. It was open season on the
Shining Path wherever members of the outlaw group assembled to conduct training sessions and plot treachery
against the state. These were no simple suspects, or ex-
convicts vindicated by the leftist courts. They were op-
posing soldiers in a war that had been raging for the best
part of three decades now, without a break.

Another difference was the simple fact of numbers.
When you faced a large encampment of guerrillas, possibly with armed support from peasants in the neighborhood, a handful of commandos wearing ski masks and
blue denim simply couldn't do the job. It needed crushing
force—with air support and heavy guns, if necessary—to
ensure a victory for law and order.

As for the preliminary move against Tristan del Sol,

Captain Menendez once again concurred with his superior that natives of the village were a treacherous, unpatriotic breed. If killing them would serve as an example to the uncommitted masses of Peru, then it would be a useful object lesson. Few were truly innocent, Menendez told himself. The sons and daughters of conspirators grew up to scheme at treason on their own.

He lost track of the scouts and raised a hand to halt the line of soldiers trailing behind him. No one spoke without permission from the officer in charge. It was an eerie scene, three dozen soldiers dressed in camouflage fatigues, all packing automatic weapons, standing in the dappled shadows of a montane forest, deathly still. A moment later, glancing back at the communications officer, Menendez got a thumbs-up signal, indicating that his scouts had made visual contact with the village of Tristan del Sol.

Menendez gestured for the others to approach him, issuing his orders in a low-pitched voice that wouldn't carry beyond their huddle on the trail. He watched their eyes, made sure each member of the company was clear on what he was supposed to do.

No prisoners.

These men had been around, and none would flinch from the unpleasant job that lay ahead. More to the point, none had a friend or relative in the vicinity who might distract him when the time came, staring down a rifle barrel, with his finger on the trigger.

Standing back, Menendez watched his troopers melt into the jungle, fanning out on both sides of the trail. They would surround Tristan del Sol in moments, draw a ring of steel around the mountain hamlet to contain its evil and, when all of them were finally in place, he would signal the attack.

Menendez moved in closer to the action while he

counted off the final moments, glancing at his wristwatch frequently to verify the time. In front of him he saw the village rooftops, lazy curls of smoke above the rusty stovepipe chimneys, scrawny dogs and dark, potbellied children littering the streets.

He drew his service pistol, thumbed the hammer back and aimed it toward the sky. His men were out there, hidden in the foliage, waiting for his signal to proceed. No sooner had he fired his one shot toward the heavens than three dozen automatic weapons started pouring fire into the village, raking dusty streets and tin-roofed hovels with a cloudburst of destructive fire.

The captain stood and watched it all, unflinching. They couldn't kill everybody from a distance, but it always helped to soften up a target prior to sending in his infantry. The mopping-up should be a relatively simple process, nothing lengthy for a place this size. Tristan del Sol had been a wide spot in the road, with fewer than one hundred full-time residents, and it was dying before his very eyes.

Menendez lit a thin cheroot, the odors of tobacco smoke and gunsmoke mingling in his nostrils. When he moved among the bullet-punctured huts and bodies in a little while, he would experience the smell of death, but it was nothing new.

They were old friends, Menendez and the Reaper. They had worked together frequently, and got along just fine. Someday, when Death came knocking on his own door, it would greet Menendez as a longtime friend.

But not this day. Not yet.

This day they would be working hand in hand.

SOUND TRAVELED in the country, but it got distorted, too. The first shot could have come from anywhere within a mile or so, and Bolan would have had no luck pursuing it…but then, all hell broke loose. It sounded like the concentrated fire of twenty-five or thirty automatic weapons, maybe more, somewhere ahead of him and slightly to the west, a small correction in his course that wouldn't cost him any extra time.

In fact, if Bolan's first guess was correct, the battle sounds would serve him as a beacon, beaming him directly to his goal.

Another klick or two, he thought, already moving toward the source of the gunfire. It didn't last long, no more than thirteen minutes from the time he checked his watch against the first shot, but it was enough. With that kind of firing, he would smell the battle site before he saw it.

The montane forest wasn't dense and stifling, like the jungles he had known in Southeast Asia or along the Amazon. He had the altitude to thank for that, along with soil, precipitation and the rest of it. He didn't have to hack his way through creeping vines and bamboo thickets, making noise enough to wake the dead, and stealthy silence was a weapon in his arsenal, as much as any gun or blade he carried.

Bolan slowed his pace when he smelled cordite on the breeze. You couldn't fire that many rounds and not expect to leave an aftertaste behind. They called it "smokeless" powder, and it fit the bill, compared to the technology of bygone days. Even so, combustion and explosions had their waste products, including vapors that were visible and-or detectable by smell.

Like now.

Brief moments after Bolan's nose identified the reek of gun smoke, he began to pick out voices calling back and forth to one another, somewhere up ahead. The voices were all male, all speaking Spanish, some of them keyed up, while others simply sounded tired or maybe bored.

It was the sound of soldiers picking over bodies on a battlefield.

He took his time advancing through the trees, alert to any sentries that the raiding party might have left behind to guard its flank. There were none, and at last he chose a tree to climb, preferring altitude for both the range of vision that it gave him and the freedom from a risk of any stragglers sneaking up behind him in the woods.

Before him, in a clearing to the northwest, he saw what once had been a peaceful-looking village, overrun with uniforms and weapons. Everywhere he looked, Bolan saw bodies on the ground, some of them women, children, here and there a shock of snowy hair denoting age. There seemed to be no living prisoners, a fact confirmed as Bolan watched the soldiers pairing off to burn the wooden houses. Moments later there was more smoke rising through the trees, a different smell as hungry flames took hold.

He waited, watching, as the officer in charge reviewed his troops, apparently congratulating them on their achievement. Most of them looked satisfied, some cocky, while a few—the older veterans, he guessed—were more blasé, the soldiers who had seen and done it all, including massacres of unarmed villagers, without regard to age or sex.

A primal rage gripped Bolan, urging him to cut loose on the troops in front of him with everything he had. He might not get them all, but he could give them hell, and then some, while they tried to bring him down. The only thing that stopped his hand from reaching for a 40 mm MECAR round was the distinctive shoulder patch the killers wore.

They were security police.

It was at times like this when Bolan questioned his resolve, his blind commitment to a rule that he would never kill a cop, regardless of the ruthless bastard's crimes. It was a point of honor with the Executioner, and yet, if he had reached the village moments earlier, while those in front of him were busy slaughtering their helpless victims, then...

Then what?

He couldn't say.

There had been situations in the past where he had knocked an officer unconscious, maybe injured one a bit, but nothing lethal. Then again, it hadn't been his fate, thus far, to walk in on a massacre in progress, with police on the dispensing end of sudden death. The foul Gestapo were police, in Hitler's Germany; would he have spared their lives at Auschwitz, Buchenwald, or Bergen-Belsen?

No.

Was this scum any better?

Maybe not.

There was a crucial difference, though, if only in the timing. He had reached the scene too late to make a difference in the outcome of the massacre, and while it was within his power to exact a price for what the killer cops had done, his mind was focused on another possibility just now.

The troops were hunting; that was obvious. He didn't think it was a mere coincidence that they were hunting north of Yauyos, at the very moment when a group of Shining Path guerrillas was supposed to be converging on the area. In fact there was a chance that someone on the hit team knew where Bolan's quarry was.

Or maybe they were just out hunting peasants, as a way to kill some time.

The best way to find out, he thought, would be to follow them and see exactly where they went.

Five minutes later Bolan had his answer, or a portion of it.

They were headed north, away from Yauyos.

Bolan gave them ample room, then climbed down from his perch and followed them.

Toward what?

The Executioner would know when they arrived, and not before.

8

The sun was going down when Mercy Hastings reached the outskirts of Tristan del Sol. She had spent time in Yauyos, trying not to be conspicuous as she picked up some new gear for the trail. The merchandise on hand was limited, but she had found a denim jacket and a canvas backpack, olive drab. The pack now held her extra ammunition and a small first-aid kit, some beef jerky and a gallon jug of bottled water. She had matches in her pocket, plus the "borrowed" flashlight, with a set of brand-new batteries. The six-inch hunting knife on Hastings's belt was also new, and razor-sharp. She had the 12-gauge loaded, with a live round in the chamber, and the safety on.

Survival training had been worse than this, she told herself, except that no one on those practice runs was really out to kill her. If she lost it here, the very best that she could hope for was a chance to kiss her ass goodbye.

She heard the shooting from a distance, fifty minutes out, and took a fix on the approximate position, moving cautiously in the direction of the sound. It seemed unlikely that the Shining Path would make that kind of racket practicing, when every constable and soldier in the country was on constant red-alert and itching for a chance to bag a few guerrilla scalps, but gunfire in the jungle could mean anything.

Correction: it meant trouble, and the only question left

was the ID of those on the dispensing and receiving ends, respectively.

She took her time, not rushing it, but not exactly dawdling, either. Hastings was alone and on unfamiliar ground, and it was only common sense for her to watch her step. Whatever had occasioned so much shooting, there were many guns involved, and she felt no great urge to find herself surrounded by that kind of firepower.

It took the better part of ninety minutes for her to locate the village after all the shooting ended, and the stench of death had edged out the smell of gun smoke by the time she reached Tristan del Sol. She spent long moments circling the burned-out village, carrying her shotgun with the safety off, prepared for anything, before she dared emerge from cover and explore the killing ground.

She couldn't say how many people had been killed here. There were thirty-five or forty scattered in the blood-soaked dust of what had once been village streets, but Hastings guessed an equal number, maybe more, had died inside their homes. Those huts and modest bungalows were all reduced to ashes now, still smoldering and giving off a sickly reek of roasted human flesh.

What kind of people would do a thing like this?

She counted lifeless children, felt the tears start in her eyes and wiped them angrily away. She wanted to believe the Shining Path had done this, something to confirm her hatred for the bastards who had seized her father, but she knew enough of Third World politics to realize that the Peruvian security police and soldiers were as capable of wholesale slaughter as their enemies. If anything, the uniformity of scattered brass around the scene—all 5.56 mm, as from M-16s—would seem to indicate official trigger-men. Outlaw guerrillas, Hastings knew, were much more likely to employ a motley arsenal of mismatched hardware on their raids, with everything from sporting arms to heavy weapons stolen from their enemies.

Whoever was responsible had marched northward when finished with the butchery. A novice tracker could have followed them with no great difficulty. There were thirty men or more, she estimated, who'd made no attempt to hide their tracks.

That kind of confidence confirmed her first impression that the killers were official, authorized for hunting humans in the area. As far as what that meant to her and to her mission, she could only guess.

If they were cops or soldiers, then it stood to reason they were hunting rebels. So was she, and Hastings saw no reason why she shouldn't take advantage of another hunter's effort if it served her purpose. She would have to watch her step, of course, look out for any rearguard spotters and avoid whatever traps the hunters might have left behind them to prevent hostile pursuit. That much was relatively easy, something she was trained for. But the rest of it, well, that could be a problem down the line.

Suppose the soldiers found what they were looking for—a Shining Path encampment in the forest—and they launched another raid, without regard for who was slaughtered in the process. Would her father pay the price for their excessive ruthlessness? What could she do to save him if it came to pass?

Not much, perhaps, but she would give it everything she had. And anyone who tried to harm her father, while she lived and had the means to stop him, would be stopped. She didn't give a damn if her potential enemy was wearing dress blues or a pair of faded denim overalls. She had a job to do, and nothing short of death would keep her from completing it.

Dusk was a passing fancy in the montane forest, where tall trees cast soothing shadows all day long, and sunlight filtered through the crowded branches like the soft rays from a neighbor's porch light. Twilight didn't linger; rather, night fell like a weighted curtain, blotting out the light.

It would be slower tracking from now on. She dared not use the flashlight more than briefly and at random intervals. One glimpse of light could easily betray her, while the flash played havoc with her night eyes, forcing her to pause and let her pupils readjust each time she switched it off.

It was slow going, but she didn't lose the trail.

She might be on a wild-goose chase, but she was hanging on until the end of the line.

KEEPING UP with the patrol was easier once darkness fell. Bolan didn't know the full extent of training offered to the security police, but they clearly hadn't been over-worked as jungle fighters. Bolan tracked them by the noise they made, as he found a parallel track and kept up the pace without breaking a sweat. It seemed unlikely that guides were leaving rearguard troops along the trail, but he would miss them now, regardless.

Moving freely through the forest, concentrating on the track with half his mind, the Executioner had time to think his options through. What would he do, for instance, if the gunners he was following weren't bound for the Shining Path encampment, after all, but simply sweeping local villages at random, killing off peasants for fun or profit? Could he stand by on the sidelines while another massacre went down, this time before his very eyes? At what point did commitment to a vague ideal become superfluous, a handicap to reason and performance of the duty he had taken on himself when he began his one-man war against the predators?

Would taking out a pack of rabid animals in uniform

somehow destroy the moral underpinnings of his cause, regardless of the provocation and their crimes? Conversely what kind of commitment to the good fight did he really have, if certain savages were guaranteed a free pass?

Uncertainty was death in Bolan's world. A fighting soldier didn't always have the answers, but he either had to find them as he went along, or fake it when the chips were down. A lucky guess could do it sometimes, but a warrior who relied on luck too much was riding for a killer fall. Where knowledge failed, in battle, grim determination sometimes had to make up for the loss. The soldiers scaling cliffs, hand over hand, on D day, didn't know how many German troops were waiting for them at the top, but they went up and killed them, anyway.

Things just worked out that way sometimes…or not.

Ideally Bolan hoped these killer cops would lead him to the Shining Path encampment, where he hoped he would find at least some clue to where the terrorists were holding Garrick Hastings. If it meant another blitz in Lima, that was fine. Whatever, he had pledged himself to solve the riddle. No one in the States expected him to guarantee that he would find the diplomat alive or bring him safely home, but privately he knew that anything less would smack of failure, haunting him to the end of his days.

And once he crossed that line, there was no turning back.

The massacre was two full hours behind them—three miles, give or take, allowing for terrain—when someone had the bright idea to pitch camp for the night. Short moments later, scavengers were fanning out in search of firewood, seemingly oblivious to any standard of security or stealth. He could have killed them easily, but concentrated on avoiding them instead, his mind made up to wait it out and see what happened next.

It galled him, but the other choice—proceeding on his own without a clear-cut destination—seemed to offer no great prospect of success. This way, at least, if he was forced to lose some time, he could rest up a bit and get a fresh start on the trail the next day. It wouldn't have been his choice, but Bolan sometimes had to play the cards as they were dealt if he had any hope at all of staying in the game.

They had a bonfire blazing now, and some of them made perfect targets, backlit by the flames, while others started pitching two-man tents around the clearing they had chosen for their campsite. When they posted sentries, only two men roamed the perimeter, so situated that the fire's light had to have spoiled their vision, while the chatter of their comrades would have made it difficult for them to hear a herd of elephants advancing through the trees.

Rank amateurs, Bolan thought. They were slick enough to sneak up on a peaceful village to gun down unarmed civilians, but they didn't have a clue about surviving in the wild, when there were hostile eyes and ears nearby.

He backed off from the clearing, found another tree and went for altitude. The fork he chose to sleep in wasn't long on comfort, but he wouldn't tumble to the ground when he dozed off, and there was zero chance of any human adversary sneaking up on Bolan while he slept. As for his wake-up call, he had no doubt the Lima detail would make noise enough to wake up Rip Van Winkle when they started breaking camp.

He was already dozing, in that twilight world between full wakefulness and deeper sleep, when something roused him, brought him back to the here and now. There was a noise emanating from the ground beneath his aerie. Bolan gripped his Steyr AUG and thumbed off the safety, prepared for anything until he satisfied himself on two key points of information.

First the noise had been produced by human beings.

Second they had no idea that he was lounging twenty feet above their heads.

In fact, he saw now, they were closing on the camp, surrounding it. He couldn't make out uniforms or faces from that angle, in the darkness, couldn't count how many stalkers were encircling the camp, but Bolan would have bet his life that they were enemies of those who sat conversing near the fire.

His confirmation came two minutes later, when the tree line all around the clearing thundered into roaring, flashing life, unleashing storms of automatic-weapons fire. Incoming bullets dropped the two sentries first, then started picking off the soldiers grouped around the fire. More sizzling rounds ripped through the pup tents, some of them already occupied, torn canvas flapping in a man-made wind from hell.

CAPTAIN MENENDEZ had been sipping coffee, staring at the bonfire, when the world blew up around him. He started to shout orders, wondering if anyone could hear or understand him in the heat of battle. Weapons flashed all along the tree line, bullets humming through the air like huge, lethal mosquitoes, while members of his hunting party shouted, cursed, died.

He was struggling to his feet when someone fell against him, staggering the captain, driving him back toward the bonfire as he fell. One arm was in the flames, he realized, and whipped it free, the sleeve of his field jacket burning like a torch. Menendez thrashed it wildly through the air, felt white-hot pain sear through his hand and wrist, before his training came back to him and he beat the flames by rolling over on his arm.

Some of his men were firing back, a hopeful sign, but they had nothing in the way of cover, while their adversaries were concealed from view, bright muzzle-flashes offering the only point of reference for anyone returning fire. Menendez knew he was a sitting duck, with leaping flames behind him, and he started to crawl from the bonfire toward the line of tents, where several of his men had turned in after finishing their rations. Three or four of them were still inside their tents, feet sticking out, and he could tell from how the canvas fluttered, shredded by incoming fire, that they wouldn't be getting up again.

Instinctively the captain looked for his communications officer. It was a hopeless notion, calling out for help; Major Padilla could send troops, but they wouldn't arrive for hours yet, assuming they began their trek before the sun came up. A waste of time, and yet he couldn't think of any viable alternative.

Menendez spotted his communications officer, facedown and limp, halfway between his own position and the tree line. There was no sign of the squat field telephone he carried everywhere. It could be in the dead man's tent, whichever one *that* was, but searching for it would be foolish, even suicidal, in the present circumstances.

Shouting orders at his men, Menendez tried to rally them. He drew his pistol, picking out a portion of the tree line nearest to him, firing at a couple of the red-orange muzzle-flashes winking there. Menendez had no reason to believe that he was scoring with his shots, but there was little more for him to do.

He wondered, for perhaps a heartbeat, whether these guerrillas were attacking him because of his assault upon the nearby village, or because he had come close to spying out their secret base. Perhaps the two had run together, self-defense and vengeance bundled into one. It mattered little, though, because the captain and his soldiers were about to be delivered into the next plane of existence if Menendez didn't come up with a miracle, and soon.

Menendez wished he were a praying man and tried to remember fragments from the Catholic masses of his childhood, but they wouldn't come. No problem, since he didn't have the candles or the holy water with him anyway.

"'Our Father, who—'"

A bullet struck the earth mere inches from the captain's face, flung dirt into his mouth, choking off his prayer before he finished the amenities. Menendez spit and cursed, kept moving like a lizard, digging with his knees and elbows.

He fired another round toward the trees, not aiming, knowing it was wasted effort even as he pulled the trigger. Still, it helped to know that he was doing something, even if it was a futile gesture.

The grenade came out of nowhere, wobbling through the darkness, silent where the guns were loud, its impact less distinctive than the sound of lifeless bodies falling to the turf. The first warning Menendez had was the explosion, fire and thunder, as the shock wave lifted him and flipped him over on his back.

He came down deaf and breathless, gasping as he struggled to inhale. Warm dampness on his inner thigh told him that he was either wounded or had wet himself. Whatever, he was still alive and capable of moving, thinking.

It was time to get away from there and try to save himself.

Menendez struggled to his hands and knees, head throbbing as if he were suffering the worst hangover in recorded history. He was aware of crimson dripping from his nostrils, wondered if the blast had damaged him internally and shrugged it off. If he was dying, there was nothing to be done about it now. As long as he could breathe and move, however, he was obligated to resist the enemy and try his best to get away.

He started crawling toward a point on the perimeter where there appeared to be no gunmen for a space of twenty-five or thirty feet. If he could make it back into the forest, find a place to hide, there was at least some hope he would be overlooked. And if he failed, if they should root him out somehow, Menendez would be no worse off than he was now, surrounded and pinned down.

The captain staggered to his feet, surprised to find the pistol still clutched in his hand. Determination still paid off, sometimes. He started for the tree line, shuffling, jerky steps that made him look as if he were intoxicated or deranged. Before he traveled twenty feet, two gunners fixed their sights on him from opposite directions, front and back, unloading six or seven rounds apiece.

Menendez never heard the shots that killed him, even though he took a while to die. The spray of bullets knocked him down, and he could feel the pistol drop from nerveless fingers as he fell. The ground was rough against his cheek and smelled of grass.

"'Our Father...art...forgive...'"

His mind wouldn't retrieve the words and images required to make the prayer coherent. Dying where he lay, Menendez gave up on the prayer and closed his eyes.

IT TOOK LESS TIME to waste a makeshift military camp than to annihilate a village, since the members of the ambush party had perhaps one-third as many targets, none of them with any kind of decent cover. Bolan watched and waited, steady on his perch, and watched the killer cops go down in twos and threes until there were no human targets left.

Somebody called out for a cease-fire, and his words

were instantly obeyed, the guns immediately falling silent.
Seconds later Bolan saw two scouts emerge from cover,
one approaching from the north, another from the east.
They moved among the dead and dying, kicking this one,
rolling that one over, bending to slit another's throat,
where signs of life remained. The cleanup was efficient,
brisk and brutal.

When the scouts were done, the other members of the
ambush party waded in and started to collect the spoils.
Weapons were the top priority, but each man took as
much as he could carry: boots and web belts, knives and
shovels, caps and jackets if they weren't soiled with
blood. Nobody went for trousers, indicating they were
pros who knew that people lost control of bowels and
bladder in the throes of violent death.

When they were finished cleaning up, the motley firing
squad formed sloppy ranks and left the clearing, heading
north. They moved with greater stealth than their late enemies, but no less speed.

He climbed from his perch and warily approached the
clearing, where the half-naked bodies sprawled like frat-
house brothers sleeping off a midterm orgy. Bolan didn't
bother checking them for signs of life; the ambush team
had done that, and he had no time to waste on dying
murderers. If there was such a thing as karma, Bolan
thought that he had seen the wheel of fate turn right before
his eyes.

"Win some, lose some," he told the corpses strewed
around the crackling fire.

There were no weapons visible among the dead. The
Shining Path guerrillas were proficient scavengers, retriev-
ing any object that could serve their cause and leaving
only what was too soiled or damaged to be worth the
effort. With the loot from thirty-odd dead soldiers, they
could clothe and arm an equal number of their own men,

maybe use the stolen shirts and caps to dress some ringers for an infiltration raid.

The forest ambush marked a change in circumstances, but it didn't alter Bolan's plan. He had been following the soldiers when they camped, and he would trail their killers now. They had to lead him somewhere, and if Garrick Hastings wasn't waiting at their destination, he could still try picking off a member of the troop and grilling him for further information.

It was worth a try. In fact it seemed to be the only game in town.

Without a backward glance, he left that place of death and started following his latest quarry to the north.

9

With nightfall Mercy Hastings's hike became a waking nightmare. She was moving rapidly toward physical exhaustion, needing sleep, but she wouldn't allow herself to rest before she overtook her quarry. After that, when she had seen whomever she was following, there would be time for her to decide on some new strategy, perhaps to get a little rest before she forged ahead.

Her stomach growled, and she retrieved a strip of jerked beef from her pack. It had the same appearance and consistency as shoe leather, but most shoes weren't salted to the point of amplifying thirst a hundred times. She chewed the beef for a while, then spit it out, disgusted with her choice. But Hastings stowed the rest for an emergency. She had to stop to take the pack off to extract her gallon jug of water, sipping lightly, just enough to cut the salt and make her tongue stop tingling.

She glanced up at the moon, just visible above the treetops, and wondered where Mike Belasko was, if he could see it—or if he would even care to take the time. She knew he was a stone professional and a remorseless killer, but she still couldn't help wondering about his human side. Did he have one? Would he accept assignments on their merit, with the hope of helping someone, or was he no better than a guided missile, aimed at targets half a world away and detonated by remote control?

Where was he at that moment? Had he managed to make any progress searching for her father?

She put the questions out of mind and concentrated on her feet. A twisted ankle would defeat her now, much less a snakebite or a booby trap. She also had to watch for snipers, though the darkness made it difficult, if not impossible, for her to do so. Hastings hoped the gunmen she was following would hold their course and give no thought to someone trailing them. If they had posted guards, and if the guards were any good at all, she could be up that famous creek without a paddle.

She used the flashlight every hundred yards or so, shielding it with her free hand, switching it on just long enough to spot signs on the trail: torn leaves and broken branches, scuff marks on the trees, where men and gear had brushed against the bark with force enough to scar it.

Hastings was tiring, but she wouldn't stop to rest. Each moment lost would give the enemy a greater lead and make it that much harder for her to keep up.

She didn't count the soldiers and security police as allies any longer. They had failed to find her father and had locked her up instead, pretending it was in her "own best interest." Hastings didn't know if they were all corrupt or simply negligent, but it amounted to the same thing either way. They were content to sit around and talk about their long war with the Shining Path, maybe go out and massacre a peasant village when they had the energy to stir out of their barracks, but she saw no evidence of any will to win. And there was definitely no concern for Yankee diplomats, beyond a fear that U.S. aid might be cut off if the authorities didn't put on some kind of dog and pony show, pretending they were on the job.

Okay.

When Hastings got her father safely home and finished serving out her brig time, maybe she would put the whole damned story in a book. That ought to raise some eyebrows on the Foreign Affairs Committee, maybe even higher up.

The trick was that before she started to write anything, she had to find her father and retrieve him from captivity, then somehow manage an escape, when both the terrorists and the authorities were breathing down her neck.

Good luck, she thought.

But it wasn't a hopeless task. She had already come this far, and Hastings wasn't willing to admit that she was on a wild-goose chase. Not yet.

As long as there was hope, there was a reason to keep trying.

Mercy Hastings cinched her pack a little tighter and walked on into the night.

IT MADE Padilla nervous, staring at the clock on the cantina wall, so he had turned his chair around and faced the bar, surrounded by his aides and bodyguards. They were in rebel country whether he admitted it or not, and common sense dictated that he watch his back—or detail someone else to watch it for him.

With the clock behind him, out of sight, Padilla found himself glancing repeatedly in the direction of his wristwatch. It was going on four hours, since he had been advised of the successful raid on Tristan del Sol. No further messages had been received, and he had other soldiers lurking in the forest to the west and east of Yauyos, waiting for a signal to proceed and keep their rendezvous. Still, no word from Menendez and his company, assigned to raze the peasant village as a kind of warm-up, then move on to find Padilla's lifelong enemies.

He should have heard from them by now, whatever they were up to. Check-ins every hour was the rule for this campaign. Menendez understood that, and he wasn't one to willfully ignore an order. On the other hand, if they had been attacked, there should have been some word, a call for help, if nothing else. Padilla couldn't even send them reinforcements if he didn't have a clue to their location.

He smelled trouble, but the situation was potentially explosive. He didn't have troops enough on hand to sweep the jungle thoroughly without some finite starting point. His men would do as they were told, but they were soldiers, not mind readers. If they had to start from scratch, hunting Menendez and his troopers in addition to the Shining Path encampment, it would clearly be too much.

Padilla needed helicopters, but for that he had to concoct a story to convince his tight-fisted superiors. The whirlybirds cost money every minute they were in the air, and sending them aloft to look for soldiers who hadn't checked in on time wasn't the kind of mission Lima would be likely to approve. Conversely, if he lied and told the brass that he had found the Shining Path's secret headquarters, the choppers would be his...but he would have to show results or face the consequences of his failure.

No. Not yet.

He knew approximately where Menendez and his troops should be, if they had marched due north from Tristan del Sol, but it was too late now for search parties. One missing company was bad enough, without involving others. If Menendez and his men were dead, there was no helping them this night. If they were still alive and had lost contact with Padilla for some reason, there was still no way for him to find them in the dark.

He started ticking off the problems that could make a rifle company lose touch with its commanding officer. A lost or damaged radio was one idea, although it seemed unlikely, short of violent contact with the enemy. Menendez and at least one other member of his company were trained to use the radio, in case the operator wound up getting killed, so that was no excuse.

What other explanation could there be?

Padilla started working on alternative solutions to his problem, just in case Menendez never called him back. If there had been no word by sunrise, he decided, then he would be justified in thinking that the captain's company had been wiped out. The Shining Path didn't take prisoners, except when they were snatching wealthy businessmen or diplomats, so he could rule out any notion that his men were prisoners of war.

The good news was that he possessed a rough idea of where the enemy encampment was supposed to be. If there was still no word by morning, when the first gray light of dawn broke in the sky, he would be sending every man he had to scour the area, with orders to continue searching until they had something to report.

Three dozen soldiers didn't simply disappear without a trace. He wouldn't go back to Lima and report that he had lost one-fourth of his command and didn't have a clue where they had gone or what had happened to them.

His reputation and career would rest upon what happened in the next few hours, and Padilla was determined to succeed at any cost. Assuming that Menendez and his troops were dead already—which seemed likely, in the circumstances—then it wouldn't hurt to wait for dawn. Let the assassins celebrate, grow overconfident and careless. When the final trap was sprung, they would be taken by surprise.

And in the meantime, all that he could do was wait.

AN HOUR into the stalk, Bolan decided that he might as well begin to trim the odds if he could pull it off discreetly. It wasn't long after that before he saw his opening.

The rebel column had no military discipline, some twenty-five or thirty men strung out along a hundred yards of trail, with no one seemingly in charge. Pure logic told him that there had to be some kind of officer up front, but that wouldn't affect his plan.

His chance came when a member of the strike team fell out to relieve himself, the others moving on without him, trusting him to find his way when he was finished. Bolan waited for the man to rise and hoist his trousers, then stepped up behind him while the rebel buttoned up his fly, the Ka-bar whispering through flesh beneath his chin. Blood fountained from the wound, propelled by air exploding from the man's lungs, but he couldn't cry out with severed vocal cords. A moment later he was resting on a bed of ferns, concealed from anyone who might return to look for him along the trail.

The column had a short lead on him, and Bolan hurried to catch up. His progress through the forest wasn't absolutely silent, but the rebels made enough noise on their own to cover any sounds of pursuit. From all appearances, they knew the local ground so well that they had no fear of an ambush.

The last rebel in line was carrying a captured M-16 A-1 and had an older M-1 carbine slung across his back, with bandoliers of ammunition hanging from his skinny shoulders. He was plodding like a farmer in the field, head down, not interested in keeping up with his companions. If he lagged a bit behind the rest, there was no one around to chastise him.

No one, that was, except the Executioner.

He couldn't risk a scuffle with the rebel, so he drew the 93-R from its shoulder rig and stepped onto the game trail. The guerilla turned, as if sensing the presence of an enemy, and unslung his rifle. Bolan fired his pistol from thirty feet away. The first round struck his target in the head, punching him to the ground. The Executioner reached the body in a flash and dragged it off the trail, concealed it hastily and went back to the hunt.

Two down, and twenty-odd to go. He didn't intend to kill them all before they reached their camp, but he would take another three or four if possible, and give the rebels something to consider when they straggled home and started counting heads. It was a risky game for small reward, but Bolan liked to stir things up whenever possible. If anything could shake an adversary's confidence, it was in his best interest to pursue that angle of attack with all deliberate zeal.

Which brought him back to contact with the marching column, coming up on number three, the new caboose. This one seemed hinky, glancing back from time to time, as if concerned about the soldiers who had lagged behind. He frowned and muttered something to himself in Spanish, but continued on another fifty yards before he paused.

Bolan could almost hear the cogwheels turning in the man's mind, deciding whether he should wait for those behind him, let them catch up on their own or maybe shout a warning to the men ahead. If he did that, the game was up. Bolan had no doubt of his own ability to dodge a dragnet in the forest, but wanted nothing to delay their progress toward the camp. It would be self-defeating if he had to fight the rebels here, and thus deprive himself of what appeared to be his only guides.

He lingered in the darkness by the trail, waiting for the guerilla to make up his mind. Another moment, and the guy turned back, retracing his steps and calling out to those who had been left behind.

He moved past Bolan, never heard the Executioner step out behind him with the Ka-bar in his hand. The man still wasn't thinking trouble. He was plainly more annoyed than worried, maybe thinking he would catch the blame if anyone got lost along the route of the march.

His mouth was opening to call them again, when Bolan sealed it with the palm of his left hand and swung the Kabar with his right, the long blade disappearing underneath his adversary's chin. Blood splashed across his hand as Bolan gave the knife a twist and felt it grate on bone, the body in his grasp gone as limp as rags.

He made his third trip off the trail, with deadweight trailing in the dirt behind him, leaving tracks that would be visible if anybody took the time to look for them. They would need light, though, and the dawn was still long hours away.

So far, so good.

The Executioner glanced back toward the trail and saw another rebel moving toward him, weapon at the ready. Bolan mouthed a silent curse and freed the silenced Uzi from its shoulder sling.

Had this one heard the other calling to their tardy comrades? Bolan didn't know, and speculation was a waste of time. Something had compelled the gunman to retrace his steps, and he was getting closer by the moment, scanning shadows to the left and right in search of comrades who had fallen out along the way.

Bolan waited five more seconds, counting off, before he stroked the Uzi's trigger and dispatched a 3-round burst from twenty feet away. The parabellum shockers took his target in the chest and punched him through a clumsy pirouette, his trigger finger clenching as he fell. The rifle had been set for semiauto, and it fired only one round, but that was one too many in the circumstances.

Bolan was already moving as the gunshot echoed through the night, alert to voices and the sound of running feet as other rebels started doubling back.

He needed space and cover, somewhere to hide while they were searching for him, short of taking on the whole platoon. Inevitably, if he dodged them, they would head back to their camp. It might extend the track by hours, but he guessed they would have nowhere else to go.

And all he had to do was stay alive until they tired of hunting him.

DIEGO FLORES GRIPPED his AK-47 tightly, waiting for his soldiers to report. They had been scouring the woods for twenty minutes, and they had still come up with nothing but the body of Ernesto Calderon. Three other men were missing from the company, but there was no sign of them anywhere.

Calderon had three bullets in his chest, and yet the only gunshot heard had been his own, apparently discharged as he was falling to the ground. As for the other missing men, they could have vanished anywhere along the three miles from the campsite where the government patrol had been wiped out.

Flores didn't feel like going back to look for them, especially if there was someone in the forest, watching him, someone whose weapon had a sound suppressor attached, from all appearances, and who was skilled enough to use it, slip away and hide before the dead man's comrades could run back and catch him in the act.

Of course, if Flores was completely honest with himself, the phantom gunman didn't have to be a superman to slip away from these young guns. They were proficient, in their way, but sneaking up on careless men and shooting them from ambush didn't take the greatest soldiers in the world. The moon was full tonight, but treetops filtered out its light and left deep shadows on the forest floor. Flores thought his men might do a better job of tracking after sunrise, but he couldn't spare that kind of time.

Reluctantly he called his soldiers back, half cringing at the way his own voice carried in the night. He wondered if the enemy was out there, watching him, the crosshairs of a sniper scope locked on his forehead as he stood fast in the middle of the trail. It made his skin crawl, and a cold sweat broke out on his face.

The others took their time about responding to his call. Their blood was up, and they were itching for revenge. When they were reassembled, though, he soon found out that none of them was interested in carrying Calderon's body back to camp. They had another two miles left to go, and Flores couldn't blame them in the circumstances. One man dead, three others missing, and there might still be an enemy out there, prepared to strike at any moment. No one wanted to be burdened with a corpse if there was fighting to be done, or if they had to run.

He compromised and had them strip Calderon's weapons, ammunition, boots and web gear, sharing the extra load among themselves. No matter what, it was an iron-clad rule that soldiers of the Shining Path never left hardware behind, if there was any way at all to save it. No one argued with the order, each of them relieved that he wouldn't be lugging a corpse back to camp.

Flores wondered if the other missing men had anything to do with killing Calderon. It would be most unusual, if so, and he was privately inclined to doubt it. Still, the possibility remained, and he could almost hope that it was true. It would solve a world of problems for him.

But it didn't make sense. There had been no quarrels in the unit that he knew of—certainly no killing arguments—and no one in his company possessed a sound suppressor. The six or seven homemade devices available were kept at headquarters, for use on special missions, under lock and key. It would be all a soldier's life was worth to get caught stealing one, and neither of the missing men possessed that kind of raw initiative.

Which meant there was at least one unknown hunter in the woods this night, perhaps still watching them, just waiting for the chance to kill again. If he had killed Calderon, then the odds were good that he had killed the other three, as well, before Calderon accidentally gave the game away.

Flores felt a sudden urge to put this dying place behind him. Snapping orders to his men, he formed them into ranks and warned them not to straggle out along the trail. They were to stay in tight formation, double-timing, until he decided otherwise.

Again no one complained.

He put two men on point and gave them twenty yards before he waved his other soldiers forward, jogging at their head. With every step he waited for a bullet to explode between his shoulder blades and bring him down, but nothing happened.

Perhaps they could make it, he decided, after they had covered half a mile.

Perhaps.

THE DISTANT GUNSHOT froze Mercy Hastings in midstride. She brought up her shotgun, even though she knew the shooter was at least a mile away. With only one shot, it was difficult to get a fix on the location, but she would have sworn that it had come from dead ahead, due north.

What did it mean?

She hesitated for another moment, waiting, but the sound wasn't repeated. Hastings told herself it might have no connection to her quest, but that was so unlikely that it almost made her laugh out loud. Two hours had passed since she'd come across the full-scale massacre of armed security police, and there was no way she could pass off *any* shooting in the woods as wholly innocent.

She had to move. Every moment wasted interfered with her chances of catching up to the war party she was tracking, made it that much more unlikely that the men—whoever they might be—would lead her to her father. She would have to keep her guard up, but she couldn't let herself be paralyzed by noises in the night.

Mercy Hastings didn't want to die, by any means, but she had made her peace with the Almighty, and she wouldn't be paralyzed by fear. If she was called upon to face long odds alone, then she would do her best, and never mind the risk. Her father was responsible for her life, and if the only way to help him out was risking it, she was prepared to take that chance.

She would have felt much better, though, if she hadn't been all alone. Some of her cronies from Fort Benning would have made a difference, even those who gave her a hard time because she was a woman "meddling" in a world of men. Most of them didn't really mean it, talking just to hear themselves, and most of those had come around when she began to beat their scores in marksmanship, P.T. and unarmed combat. They respected her, had come to see her as a person—as a soldier—and if some would never quite adjust to that, they were a dwindling minority.

But Hastings had no friends beside her at the moment. She was on her own, not lost, but getting there, preparing for a face-off with a force of unknown size and capability.

She fought an urge to use the flashlight, took a firm grip on her shotgun and moved forward, hunting deadly strangers in the dark.

10

Constantion Chavez was troubled. Rumors had been circulating around headquarters all afternoon about some "big event," and Serafin Padilla had gone missing prior to lunchtime. Normally the major's absence would have come as a relief to Chavez, but he worried that Padilla might have some trick up his sleeve, a new outrage against the peasantry he always viewed as a reserve force of the Shining Path.

It took the best part of the afternoon for him to pin down the rumors. Chavez had eyes and ears inside Padilla's command, as the major no doubt had spies watching Chavez. Paranoia was an occupational hazard for the men and women who fought organized terrorism on a daily basis, amplified and escalated by dissension in the ranks. Chavez knew that Padilla longed to see him fired, or worse, and anything the captain did to head that off was simple self-defense.

Six phone calls later, he was standing at a market stall on Avenida Roosevelt eating a *chorizo* sandwich, when his contact sidled and placed his order with the cook. Two minutes later, a spicy, precooked sausage had been forked onto a bun with onions and a dash of *jabañera* peppers. To the uninitiated, it was almost lethal, ruining the taste buds for a day or two, at least.

As for Chavez, the food reminded him of home.

When he spoke at last, Chavez spoke from the corner

of his mouth, hoping it matched the chewing motion of his jaw.

"What did you find out?" He cut straight to business. The amenities were normally reserved for friends and other people he respected.

"You were right," the informant said. "There are rumors of a hostile presence north of Yauyos. I could get no details other than the fact that he took most of a battalion with him. If the rumors are correct, he might have stumbled on a major base camp for the Shining Path."

That, or something else, Chavez thought. It would be just like the major to locate the Yankee hostage, stage a hasty raid and slaughter anything that moved, describing any casualties as rebels. If the hostage suffered for it, even died in the attempt to save him, that was simply life in wartime. Anything that helped Padilla in his personal career was fair, regardless of the rules.

Chavez could sympathize with his old adversary, to a point. Frustration was a daily fact of life for the defensive team in a guerrilla war. They sat and waited for the unseen enemy to make a move, then scrambled to react when it was already too late. Proactive efforts typically inflamed the populace, without achieving much.

"When did they leave?" the captain asked.

"Nobody knows for sure. Sometime before eleven."

Padilla's people would have reached Yauyos by now and started their sweep. Chavez was running far behind the pack, and there was little he could do to help himself catch up. The major's field trip might turn out to be a waste of time, some private fishing expedition. On the other hand, if he had found the missing American diplomat...

Chavez wished that he had a contact number for the man who called himself Belasko. The American would want to know about Padilla's war games, not to mention

Mercy Hastings. Chavez cursed again and stared with pent-up fury at his silent telephone, as if his glare could make it ring.

"What kind of transport did they take?" he asked, returning to the here and now.

"The usual," his contact told him. "Jeeps and trucks."

Chavez suppressed a smile. He had one edge, at least, if he was forced to move in an emergency. The helicopters presently available would carry twenty-seven men, not counting flight crews. He would be outnumbered by Padilla's force, but if he struck with the advantage of surprise...

Chavez caught himself and frowned. He couldn't go to war against his own superior. His men would mutiny and turn their guns on *him*—some of them, anyway—before he had a chance to pull it off. And if he won, or simply managed to survive such an engagement, how would he explain it to the brass? Chavez knew that he would be lucky to escape with life in prison on a treason charge.

He would require conclusive evidence that members of Padilla's team were murdering civilians on the major's orders, and it still might not be adequate to bring the man down. However, if the American hostage was involved, a threat of damaging relations with America, from whence the dollars flowed, Chavez might have a chance.

"What else?" he asked the spy.

"Nothing."

"All right. I'll call you later."

"Yes."

Chavez left first, alert to any sign that he was being followed but finding none. The spy would wait another ten or fifteen minutes, to protect himself, and then go back to work.

The captain, meanwhile, had plans to make. He needed twenty-five trustworthy men, whom he could place on standby, to depart from Lima on a moment's notice. He would also need the paperwork required for taking up the helicopters, without tipping off Padilla's die-hard friends among the brass.

It would require some ingenuity and nerve, but he could pull it off.

In fact the captain had no choice.

DIEGO FLORES HEAVED a sigh of relief when the sentries from camp met his column. He was panting, near exhaustion from the hectic pace of double-timing over rugged ground. His legs felt like two wooden posts, and it was all that he could do to keep from groaning at the sharp pain in his side. The taste of victory had turned to bitter ashes in his mouth.

As far as he could tell, they had sustained no further losses on the long run back to camp, but he wouldn't be sure until he lined up his soldiers and counted heads. That done, Flores would have to face the part he truly dreaded: checking in with his supreme commander and reporting mixed results.

Flores surveyed his raiding party, found that only four were missing and instructed them to stash their newly liberated weapons in the common arsenal. He spent another moment with the sergeant of the guard, describing what had happened on the trail. It seemed improbable that anyone had followed them, but one could never tell.

He wished that he had time to take a shower, maybe eat a meal, but he couldn't afford to stall with Aguillar. He would present the good news first, mention their losses in an offhand way, as if four men were of no consequence. It would go badly for him that they hadn't killed or captured their assailant, but he thought perhaps he might be able to persuade his chief that a quarrel had broken out between the stragglers, three men killing one and running for their lives. Someone would have to count the silencers, explain the lack of sound if all were present and accounted for.

Instead of stalling the inevitable, Flores went directly to Aguillar's quarters. It was late, but lights were burning in the hut, a rifleman on duty at the door. The sentry knocked and went inside, returned a moment later and relieved Flores of his rifle prior to waving him across the threshold.

"So," Aguillar greeted him without preamble, "it went well?"

"We found the butchers from Tristan del Sol," Flores replied. "They were camping in the forest. They will not be going home again."

"How many were there?"

"Thirty-five," Flores answered.

"Ah, a major victory."

"Yes, Chief. We bring rifles, ammunition, hand grenades, new boots, a few undamaged uniforms."

"You have done well, Diego."

"Thank you." The soldier cleared his throat self-consciously. "There is one other thing."

"I'm listening."

"As we were coming back…"

"Go on, Diego."

Flores swallowed hard and let it out. "There was a gunshot on the trail," he said. "One of my men was killed. Three others from the rear guard disappeared."

"Explain yourself." Aguillar's voice had taken on a cutting edge.

"We heard the shot and found one man—Ernesto Calderon—dead on the trail. Three other men were missing."

"Did you look for them?"

"Yes, Chief. They were nowhere to be found."

"And you believe one of them shot the other man?"

Flores felt the rush of color to his cheeks. His head was spinning, but he hadn't been invited to sit. "It's difficult to say," he muttered lamely.

"Why?"

"Ernesto had been shot three times. The shot we heard came from his rifle as he fell."

"You did not hear the other shots?"

"There was no sound. I swear it."

"So, the shooter used a silencer."

"He must have, Chief."

"Were you issued silencers, Diego?"

Flores shook his head. "No, sir."

Rising from behind his camp chair, Aguillar went to the door and stuck his head outside, spoke softly to the guard on duty, and came back to his seat.

"We'll soon find out if any silencers are missing from the arsenal. Did you attempt to find the man or men responsible?"

"I did. We searched the woods in all directions, for a hundred meters. It was dark, but we searched thoroughly. We could find nothing, no one."

"So, you gave it up and came back here." The leader's voice was mellow, reasonable, but there was a hint of something dangerous behind his eyes.

"Yes, Chief. What else could we do?"

"You could make sure that no one followed you, for one thing." There was sudden venom in Aguillar's voice. "Instead you might have led the killers here, directly to my doorstep."

Flores suddenly felt ill. He raised both hands, as if in self-defense, though Aguillar had made no move in his direction, yet.

"No, Chief, we were careful. I'm certain no one followed us."

"Did you leave spotters on the trail to watch your back?"

"Well, I..."

"Or string up booby traps?"

"I didn't think—"

"Exactly!" Aguillar was on his feet now, leaning close to Flores, shouting in his face. "You didn't think! And now, because of thoughtless negligence, you have endangered all of us!"

"Please, Chief—"

"Please? Please what?"

The phrase *Don't kill me* came to mind, but Flores bit his tongue and settled for "Accept my most sincere apology. I'll take the men back out and search the trail. We won't come back until we find the others or discover what became of them."

"It's too damned late for that!" Aguillar said. "If anyone was tracking you, they're here already. What you will do is report immediately to the sergeant of the guard and place yourself at his disposal. I am doubling the guard at once, before a stray battalion of security police drops in to say hello."

"They would have killed us on the trail," Flores said. "Why would they allow us to proceed?"

"To see where you were going, idiot! Perhaps one of your dead or missing soldiers spotted them, and they were forced to strike before he warned the column. Had you thought of that?"

"No."

"No. I didn't think so."

Aguillar moved toward a table in the corner of the hut and poured himself a drink. When he had drained the glass, he turned and looked surprised to find Flores watching him.

"Are you still here?"

"No, sir."

"Good."

Flores left the hut, grateful to be alive, and went to find the sergeant of the guard.

BY 1:00 A.M., Major Padilla had already given up on sleep. He could not make his mind slow down, no matter how he tried. There was sufficient alcohol on hand to do the trick, but getting drunk would be the worst thing he could do. It would go badly for him, if a call came in from his patrol, and he wasn't available to answer. That would never do.

In all sincerity, Padilla didn't think his soldiers would be calling. Not this night, not ever. He had already resigned himself to the idea that they were dead. If there was any other explanation, he would certainly have heard from them by now. By now they could have walked back from Tristan del Sol and well beyond, if they were fit for travel and their radio was simply broken.

No. His men were dead. Padilla knew it in his heart.

And if his men were dead, it meant they had collided with the Shining Path sometime after they razed the village north of Yauyos. It was vindication of Padilla's theory, in a way, and it would give his other troops a starting point when they resumed the hunt at dawn.

But they had hours yet before the new search could begin. It galled Padilla, wasting so much time, but he would be an idiot to send his men out now, when it was pitch-dark in the forest, and they could be walking into certain death. There was no profit for him in disaster, throwing lives away without result. He had to see the job done properly, or he would wish they hadn't started it at all.

It was amazing how the time dragged when his hands were tied. Major Padilla was a man of action, even though he left most of it to his various subordinates these days. He hated sitting still when there were traitors to be rooted out and punished, rebels to be hunted down and killed. Each moment wasted was a moment he would never have again, an opportunity unrealized. He could have stayed in Lima and directed the assassination teams to special targets, chipping constantly at the Shining Path infrastructure, if he had but known they would encounter difficulties in the bush.

Still, there was hope that he could pull it off, a major victory against the peasant scum who had been flaunting law and order for the better part of thirty years. It was one thing to jail a handful of the movement's leaders, as was done in 1992, and quite another thing to crush the officers in charge, together with substantial numbers of their men. That kind of victory would rock the Shining Path to its foundations and prevent a swift regrouping under standby leadership.

Or, so Padilla hoped.

If not then he would have to find some way to put a brave face on his failure when he got back to the office. There were ways to gloss things over, if he really tried, but an excuse was still no substitute for victory.

He switched on the lamp by his cot and sat up stiffly, rolling his shoulders to work out a cramp. The sudden glare of light sent roaches scurrying for cover, and Padilla cursed them with a bitterness he normally reserved for human beings.

Had it been a grave mistake that brought him to this place? He recognized the limits of his zeal, in human terms, and knew that sometimes he expected too much from his soldiers, even from himself. Still, how could he have let the golden opportunity slip through his fingers without grasping it and holding on?

Impossible.

Padilla still thought this could be his moment in the sun, regardless of the fate that had befallen his initial probe. The soldiers had succeeded in their first objective, wiping out Tristan del Sol. Beyond that, they had been instructed to make contact with the enemy—and once again they had apparently succeeded, to a point. The fact that they hadn't survived the contact was irrelevant, as long as those who followed after them were able to correct the error and emerge victorious.

Padilla took his pistol from the nightstand and began to fieldstrip it. The pointless exercise absorbed some of his nervous energy and let him focus on what had to be done at sunrise, when his strike force took the field. Their first priority would be to find the missing men, alive or dead, and, if they had been killed, as he believed, to find out where the killers went. It sounded like a relatively simple tracking job, all things considered, and he hoped they would have better luck the following day.

The leaders of the Shining Path had much to answer for. Padilla knew that he could never make them suffer adequately for the havoc they had wreaked throughout his homeland, all the years of carnage, stretching back to when he was a young man, with his whole life still ahead of him. The bastards had, in essence, robbed Padilla of the life he might have had—perhaps a wife, and children, if his work had been less brutal, more secure.

He couldn't make them suffer thirty years of pain before they died, but he would do his best, and try to make their final moments hell on earth. If their destruction helped him to advance a few rungs higher on the ladder of command, they owed him that and more.

It was the very least that they could do.

THERE WAS NO LIGHT inside the hut where Garrick Hastings was confined, one ankle shackled to the steel frame of a cot, which in its turn was bolted to the wooden floor. If he was strong enough, there was a possibility that he could rip the bolts out of the floor and thereby free himself, but such a move would certainly make noise enough to rouse the guard who stood outside his door around the clock.

Hastings had started losing track of time. He didn't think a week had passed since his abduction, but he was no longer sure. For the first few days he was locked up in a room devoid of windows, with his wristwatch taken by his captors. It had started then, the blurring of successive hours and days in a surrealistic flow, when all he really had to do was sleep or worry. Later, when they put a blindfold on him and transported him to this place, miles from anywhere, he had a chance to see the sun rise in the morning and go down at dusk, but he was already confused by then, disoriented in his sense of time and losing track of days.

No one had questioned him since he was taken from Miranda's flat, and while the silent treatment had confused Hastings at first, he quickly came to terms with it and felt a measure of relief that he wasn't regarded as some kind of secret agent for the CIA. In fact, he knew a spy—Ray Neary, at the embassy—but everybody knew that he was working for the Company, one of those open secrets that allowed the cloak-and-dagger game to run forever without any major interruptions.

As for Hastings, early on he had resigned himself to the role of a silent bargaining chip in some diplomatic power play. He knew his captors were guerrillas of the Shining Path, the only rebel group of any consequence now operating in Peru. Their general program was a left-wing antigovernment campaign, including opposition to America's ongoing foreign aid to the regime in power. Hastings guessed that his abduction had to be part of some attempt to make the U.S. cut off funds and military hardware to Peru, which had about as much chance of succeeding as a note to Santa Claus. The Powers That Be in Washington wouldn't negotiate with terrorists for the release of one man who could be replaced by any of a thousand hungry gofers in D.C.

Which meant that, barring miracles, he was as good as dead.

Hastings had come to terms with that thought on his second morning in captivity. He wasn't looking forward to the moment of his death, but neither was he terrified. He had outgrown religion in his teens, had no belief in hellfire or the Pearly Gates, but there was still a sense of sadness and regret. He would have wished to see his daughter one more time and have a chance to say goodbye, to tell her that he loved her. Given half a chance, he would have chosen life, but since the choice wouldn't be his to make, he had resigned himself to die with dignity.

The sound of excited voices in the yard outside his hut roused Hastings from his bunk. The camp was normally a quiet place at night—or had been, for the short time he had been there—and the new commotion made him wonder what was happening. He picked up bits and pieces from the words of gunmen passing by his prison hut, enough to figure out that someone from their troop had disappeared in circumstances they considered strange or ominous. The camp was going on alert, with fresh guards posted to prevent a sneak attack.

He was about to lie back down when someone snapped an order to the guard outside his door, and Hastings saw the door sweep open to admit a pair of men in jungle uniforms. One bore a lamp and he placed it on the table in the middle of the room before he left the hut and closed the door behind him. His companion, slender, dark, athletic looking, with a pistol on his hip, spent several moments staring at the prisoner before he spoke.

"How are you feeling, Mr. Hastings?"

"Like a prisoner."

"An unavoidable condition, I'm afraid." The stranger's smile stopped short of mocking him, but only just.

"Assuming you're a kidnapper, I guess that's right."

"I am a revolutionary, sir. You might have heard my name. I am Alonzo Aguillar."

The top man. Hastings said, "My work deals more with foreign trade. I don't have lots of contact with the military side."

"No matter. Your employers know my name quite well, I promise you."

"So, what's the deal? Am I supposed to be exchanged for some concession from the States, or what?" He kept his fingers crossed behind his back, still hoping that the fact that he was still alive had to count for something.

"I wish it was that simple, Mr. Hastings. Sadly your beloved government does not negotiate with freedom fighters. I believe you are aware of standard policy in that regard."

"It rings a bell, now that you mention it."

"So, it would seem your value as a hostage is severely limited."

"I guess you'd better let me go, then," Hastings said.

The rebel leader smiled. "A sense of humor in adversity is one thing I admire about Americans. You think you own the world, but you can still laugh—what is the correct expression?—when the chips are down."

"We try."

"On a more solemn note, there is a possibility that an attempt might be made to free you sometime in the next few days."

"Oh, yes?"

"They won't succeed, but I thought it was only fair to warn you in advance of what will happen if they try."

"Which is?"

"You will be killed at once, as an example to all fascists who defy the Shining Path."

"Well, thanks for sharing that."

"My pleasure."

"May I ask one thing before you go?"

"Of course."

"If I'm no good to you for trading, what's the point? I mean, why bother in the first place?"

"You will serve us well," Aguillar said, "when it is time."

It was amazing, Hastings thought, that he could hear his own death sentence without breaking down. Perhaps a part of him had always known that it would end this way.

"Well, then, I guess there's only one thing I can say."

"Which is?"

"Go fuck yourself."

The rebel leader blinked at him, then smiled before he picked up the lantern and turned back toward the door.

"Americans," he said, chuckling. "Not afraid of anything. I hope your nerves are steady, Mr. Hastings. I look forward to remembering you as a man."

11

The camp took Mercy Hastings by surprise. She had gained time since passing by the dead man on the trail, intuitively understanding that the men she sought were running now. From whom or what, she couldn't say, but she told herself that anyone who killed a member of the Shining Path could only be her friend.

That was naive and oversimplified, of course, but she was in a hurry. Something told her that the culmination of her search was rushing toward her now, a climax she couldn't escape, but rather hastened to embrace. She had no way of knowing if her father was nearby, if he was even still alive, but someone in the Shining Path could tell her—*would* tell her—before another day was out.

In her distraction, Mercy almost stumbled on the compound's outer guards. She heard their voices just in time, and thanked her lucky stars that no one had advised the men to keep their mouths shut while they were on watch. She went off the trail and took her time on the approach, crept up the perimeter unseen and kept her finger on the shotgun's trigger as she scanned the layout of the camp.

Some thought had gone into the compound's preparation. Here and there, where larger trees were cut away, the treetops had been kept in place, suspended from stout cables like the husks of giant moths caught in a spiderweb. A camou net, slung forty feet above the forest floor, completed the illusion and secured the base camp from exposure via aerial photography. An infrared device could still track body heat, warm engines, cooking fires, but it wouldn't provide the sky-high watchers with a precise head count or incisive details of the base.

The camp was roughly square, some ninety yards on each side. Four bungalows had been constructed out of lumber, roofed in corrugated metal, while the bulk of those who occupied the compound slept in tents. A fire was burning in the middle of the camp, but there appeared to be no generator, no electric lights beyond the flashlights several soldiers used to find their way around. The guards patrolled in outer darkness, studying the trees with narrowed eyes. She counted fifteen sentries, and decided she could find a way inside the camp—but first she had to know where she was going, what she would be looking for.

Two of the bungalows had riflemen outside, positioned to watch the doors. One of the guarded bungalows showed lamplight through the windows, soldiers moving in and out as if some kind of meeting were in progress, while the other sat in darkness, isolated and ignored. If there were any prisoners in camp, smart money said they would be found inside the second guarded bungalow.

Of course, she told herself, it could turn out to be the compound's arsenal, but were the soldiers so untrustworthy that guns and ammunition needed guards around the clock? It didn't scan, and she decided that the hut was worth a look, regardless of the risk involved.

With that decision made, she started working on the mechanics of the penetration. They had played these games in basic training, and beyond, field exercises where you had to creep past sentries in the darkness—or in daylight—and secure a certain goal to pass the test. She knew the moves, but it had never been real life-or-death before. This time her life was riding on the line, and Hastings wasn't even sure if she would find her father in the camp. She could be risking everything she had on a pathetic, futile exercise.

She circled the perimeter until she found a point directly opposite the hut that was her target. It was fifty feet away, perhaps a trifle less, but most of that was over open ground, where she would make an easy target for the enemy. In other circumstances, with some backup on her side, she would have called for a diversion, but she didn't have the hardware or support troops to distract the nearest sentries from their posts.

Which meant that she would have to make her way inside the camp by stealth.

The guards on the perimeter were situated roughly eighty feet apart, by Hastings's calculation. That put forty feet between her and the nearest shooter when she made her move, between the two who flanked the target bungalow. She had a choice of creeping in or rushing, and she knew that any sudden movements were more likely to attract attention from the men whom she was trying to evade.

Which meant that she would have to crawl.

No problem. Crawling on her belly had been one of the first exercises taught in boot camp. Hastings lay on her stomach, with the shotgun cradled in her arms, beneath her chin, the muzzle pointed to her left. If she was forced to use the gun, the sentry on her left was history; that much she promised herself. The rest of it was simple locomotion, lizard style, the action concentrated in her elbows, shoulders, hips and knees. She took it slowly, thankful for the grass beneath her that would minimize the scraping sounds where her body met the earth.

It seemed to take forever, one move at a time, pausing to glance in each direction every time she drew a breath. The feeling of exposure set her teeth on edge, like one of those weird dreams where she was walking through a crowded shopping mall and suddenly discovered she was nude. It felt like that, without the tingle of excitement that inevitably came with such a dream. If someone caught her there, the penalty wasn't embarrassment, but sudden death. It took only one glance from either sentry, to the left or right, and she was gone.

Her heart was hammering when Hastings reached the shadow of the bungalow and gave herself a moment's grace in which to rest. She waited for her pulse to slow, still checking out the guards on the perimeter, not free of them until she edged around the corner of the building, out of sight.

And faced another sentry.

There would be no eluding that one. She would have to take him out, and silently, or she would never see what lay inside the hut. One sound, and every soldier in the camp would be on top of her in seconds flat.

She crept around the corner, rose into a crouch and drew her hunting knife.

MACK BOLAN HUDDLED twenty feet above the forest floor, stretched out along a sturdy tree limb, checking out the Shining Path's forest hideaway. He watched the soldiers come and go, crunched numbers in his head and came to the conclusion that he would be facing odds of sixty-five or seventy to one when he began his probe. One false step anywhere along the way, and he would be as good as dead.

He still had no idea if Garrick Hastings was confined within the camp, but he had ruled out any of the canvas tents as quarters for a hostage. None of them was physically secure, none guarded, none the kind of holding cell most terrorists would allocate to a distinguished prisoner.

Which left the wooden bungalows.

He wrote two off as storage, seeing that they stood unguarded, while a third—the well-lit one, with soldiers traipsing in and out—was clearly the command post. That left one, near the perimeter to Bolan's left, which might—or might not—house a prisoner. He studied it, the guard outside who kept his rifle slung, its muzzle pointed at the ground, and wondered whether it could really be that easy.

Getting in would be no simple task, of course, and coming out again—with Garrick Hastings, if the diplomat was even there—would almost certainly mean facing down those hostile guns. He weighed the odds and wondered whether Hastings had the speed, much less the nerve, to sprint through flying bullets and survive.

There was only one way to find out.

He scrambled down the tree trunk, crouching at its base and spent another moment making sure that no sound of his swift descent had carried to the nearest guards. When he was satisfied on that score, Bolan started moving to his right, away from the hut he had marked as his target, circling around the camp's perimeter in the direction of the motor pool.

The compound had only four vehicles: two military-style jeeps, one ancient truck and a Suzuki trail bike. They were parked close together on the east side of the compound, snug beneath a double layer of camou netting. Bolan checked for guards in the vicinity, found none closer than fifty feet and took advantage of the shadows, gliding in to crouch beside the flatbed truck.

It took five minutes to secure the plastique charges where he wanted them, underneath the flatbed's cab, against the fuel tanks of the jeeps, wedged in between the trail bike's gas tank and the compact motor. Each was fitted with a radio-remote detonator, keyed to the trigger on Bolan's combat harness, so that one touch of a button would ignite the charges, taking out four vehicles at once.

And in the process, it would give the Executioner one hell of a diversion for his move against the sentry posted on the darkened bungalow.

He checked the sky against his watch, deciding he had roughly forty minutes before the first gray light of dawn broke through the trees. The timing wasn't Bolan's preference, by any means. He would have much preferred to make the raid in darkness, with sufficient night remaining to assist his getaway, but it didn't seem feasible for him to hang around the camp all day and wait for sundown to attempt his move.

If Garrick Hastings *was* inside the camp, his life was still at risk each moment that he spent in custody with soldiers of the Shining Path. The last thing Bolan needed was to stall around and let the terrorists break camp, or possibly decide to execute their hostage after they considered what had happened on the trail the previous night.

There would be no time like the present for the Executioner to make his move.

He let the darkness cover him as he began the walk back to his target, moving toward a date with death.

THE SCUFFLING SOUND outside his prison, followed by a heavy thump against the door, brought Garrick Hastings to his feet. The short hairs on his nape were bristling, the first time in his life that he had known they really *did* stand up, and while he felt an urge to run and hide, the shackle on his leg prevented him from moving more than three feet from his cot.

Another moment passed before the door swung open, and a strange hunched figure lurched across the threshold. Hastings waited, scarcely breathing, as the door was closed again. He heard some heavy object slither to the floor, and then a flashlight blazed directly in his face, forced him to close his eyes against the sudden glare.

"Daddy!"

It was a breathless whisper, but he recognized the voice at once.

"Mercy?"

It was impossible, but there she was, in front of him, the flashlight turned to show her face and cast her shadow on the ceiling.

He reached for her, but she stepped back. "My hands are wet," she said, and showed him with the flashlight.

Blood.

Behind her, a dead man dribbled crimson on the floor, his throat slashed deep enough to give his head an awkward cant. His eyes were open, staring blankly back at Hastings from the pale, slack face.

"What are you doing here, for Christ's sake?" Even in his shock, he took care not to raise his voice.

"I came to get you."

"But—"

"There's no time now. Let's go."

"I can't," he said.

"Why not?"

"My leg," he told her, waiting for the flashlight's beam to puddle at his feet.

"Who has the key?" she asked.

"I haven't got a clue."

She turned away, walked over to the dead man and crouched beside him, turning out his pockets. He was carrying no keys, but Mercy found a long, bone-handled switchblade, which she slipped into her sock.

"We'll have to try another way," she said, returning to her father with a hunting knife in hand.

"What are you doing, Mercy?"

"Have a seat, okay?"

He did as he was told and held the flashlight for her, screening it as much as possible, while Mercy started gouging at the wood around the leg of the cot where the shackle was attached. His eyes kept darting back in the direction of the doorway, wondering how much time would elapse before somebody noticed that the guard was missing from his post and came to check it out.

One shot, one warning cry, and they were both as good as dead.

He was about to mention that they had no time to spare, when Mercy said, "Stand up, please."

Hastings rose and watched her lift the corner of the cot enough to slip the dull ring of his shackle underneath. The chain was roughly eighteen inches long.

"I can't unlock this, and we don't have time to cut the chain," she said. "You'll have to let it drag, or find some way to carry it."

He stooped and took the free end of the shackle in his hand. The chain was so short that he couldn't straighten while holding it, and Hastings knew he would resemble Quasimodo walking, much less running for his life. Still, if there was no other way—

"No good," his daughter said. "Try this."

She took the free end of the shackle from him and began to wind the chain around his calf and shin, but loosely, leaving room to tuck the empty cuff in after several turns.

"How's that?"

He walked across the room and back again. His leg felt heavy, but it wouldn't slow him that much if he could only concentrate with grim determination.

"Fine," he said.

"It may come loose and trip you up."

"I'll watch it, thanks."

"Okay." She went back to the dead man, took his automatic rifle and the bloodstained bandolier of ammunition draped across his chest. Returning to her father, Mercy handed him the gun and asked, "Can you fire one of these?"

"I think so." It was years since he had fired a gun, and that had been a double-barreled 12-gauge, shooting skeet.

She cocked the rifle for him and made sure the safety wasn't on. "It's ready now," she said. "Don't touch the trigger unless you have a target. If you have to do something, do it like you mean it."

"Right, okay. Mercy—"

"No time," she said and rose on tiptoes, kissing him lightly on the cheek. "We're out of here."

He watched his daughter moving toward the door, feelings of wonder, pride and fear all jumbled up inside.

"Sounds good to me," he said.

THE SUDDEN ROAR of gunfire startled Bolan. He was halfway to his jumping-off point when it hit the fan. He ducked instinctively before he realized that he hadn't been seen. No one was shooting at him. He wasn't the target.

The rapid-fire explosions ran together. He identified two shotgun blasts, the rest of it high-powered autofire or semiautomatic. It was over in an instant—two, three seconds, tops—and Bolan heard a woman crying out in Spanish.

"*¡No fueren mas! No fueren, por favor!*"

He slung the Steyr and found a tree that would supply him with the necessary view of what was happening inside the camp. When he was thirty feet aloft, he saw a knot of soldiers clustered in front of what he took to be a prison hut. A few of them struck out with gun butts at a pair of captives in the middle of the ring. It was too dark for Bolan to make out the faces from that distance, even if his view hadn't been partially obscured.

An officer was running across the compound, shouting at his soldiers, shoving them aside as he bulled through the human ring, two bodyguards to back him up. Bolan got his first glimpse of the captives as the officer in charge confronted them, with flashlights glaring in their faces. Mercy Hastings was bruised and battered, but apparently unscathed by bullets. Kneeling at her side was an older man whom Bolan recognized immediately from his passport photo as Mercy's father. There was fresh blood soaking through the left sleeve of his shirt, where one or more rounds from the enemy had torn his flesh.

There was a knot in Bolan's stomach, causing him to grimace. He was reaching for the fire-control switch on his belt when he thought twice and drew his hand back from the doomsday button.

If he blew the charges now, there would be chaos in the camp, all right, but Mercy and her father were surrounded by a score of jumpy gunmen, any one of whom might panic when the plastique blew and kill them both without an order from the brass. Assuming they survived the first few seconds of a blitz, he was in no position to be useful, at the moment, from his perch above the camp. Disarmed, one of them wounded, they would need hands-on assistance to escape. That meant he had to climb down from on high and find another vantage point from which to strike.

Before he made the move, though, Bolan realized that he was swiftly running out of time. Gray dawn was breaking in the east, and Bolan's chances of a simple in-and-out would vanish with the darkness. Even if he blew the motor pool, a daylight raid would still entail more risk than striking from the midnight shadows. Worse yet, Mercy's efforts to release her father had the compound on alert, the soldiers armed and prowling, braced for trouble.

He forced himself to watch and wait while Mercy and her father were manhandled back inside the prison hut. A moment later two men cleared the threshold, carrying a third between them, limp in death. He gave the woman credit for proceeding that far, taking out one of the opposition, but she had been overmatched. The fact that she was being kept alive, at least for now, was good news for the Executioner, but it would be no easy task to free two prisoners instead of one.

It crossed his mind to wonder how Mercy had escaped from Lima, where she was supposed to be confined pending her deportation to the States, but there was no point puzzling over that when he had more important problems on his plate. There was a chance that Captain Chavez and his men had missed her, off the top, or that they had underestimated her resolve. If he succeeded in extracting Mercy and her father from the camp, there would be time enough to find out how she managed to elude the crack security police. Right now his mind was focused on the grim mechanics of extraction, weighing odds and options, looking for the path of least resistance, knowing it was often smoothed by flowing blood.

As long as Mercy and her father were alive, he had a chance to take them out of there, but he didn't appreciate the odds when it came down to leading unarmed prisoners past hostile guns, especially if the man was injured now. No matter what he tried, there was a decent chance that one or both of them would die, and Bolan would have failed, whether he made it out alive or not.

He needed something in the nature of a serious distraction, well beyond the charges he had planted in the motor pool, and for that, he needed a means of communication with the outside world. In which case...

Bolan scanned the camp again and found what he was looking for. It would be difficult, with daylight breaking, but the prospect brought the fifty-year-old motto of the Seabees back to mind: The Difficult We Do at Once. The Impossible Takes a Little Longer.

He made his move before dawn had a chance to drive the last of the nocturnal shadows from their place among the trees, a silent wraith circling the camp's perimeter and homing on the target, which, he hoped, wouldn't be too well guarded.

"HIS DAUGHTER." Aguillar didn't know whether he should laugh or scream. He settled for a simple statement. "I'm impressed."

The woman stared at him with bloody murder in her eyes. No mere expression, either, after she had killed the sentry single-handed, nearly severing his head. She was unarmed now, stripped of shotgun, pack and hunting knife, hands bound behind her back. The diplomat's flesh wound was bound with cloth, a graze and nothing more, no threat to life unless it should become infected.

The two of them had nearly pulled it off. A woman and her father. How would that have struck Aguillar's critics in the revolutionary movement when they heard the news? His fearsome reputation was the only thing that kept him in control of the organization, driving would-be rivals into exile or an early grave, but it could all come tumbling down around his ears if he allowed himself to be perceived as weak or negligent.

"What are you in America?" he asked the woman.

"I'm a soldier."

"Ah." That fit, though Aguillar wasn't aware that the Americans prepared their women for an active role in combat. "So," he said, "it seems that I have two guests now."

"Two prisoners," the woman replied.

"It's all the same. Perhaps, with two of you—and one

so young—your government may reconsider its position on negotiations, yes?''

"Don't hold your breath."

"Of course, you might be right. Still, it is worth a try. And in the meantime, I must ask how you were able to locate our little hideaway."

"It wasn't hard. A blind man could have found the trail your goons left in the woods."

He let the insult pass. "Most blind men wouldn't be in the location at the proper time," he said. "That must be more than a coincidence."

"The word was out in Lima," Mercy Hastings told him, seeming glad that she could wound him with the news. "Big doings with the Shining Path, up north of Yauyos. Half the country knows by now."

"Yet you came on your own," Aguillar stated.

"I'm what you might call unofficial," she replied.

"And you were fortunate enough to spot my soldiers after they were finished with the butchers from Tristan del Sol."

"See one butcher, you've seen them all."

The rebel leader smiled. "And it was you who killed my men along the trail?"

She blinked at that, recovered instantly and said, "That's right."

"Three men, I think."

"That's right."

"But, no. I am mistaken. It was four."

"Whatever." Angry color suffused her cheeks.

"I should inquire about your other weapon."

Mercy stared at him, uncomprehending, silent.

"No response?" He smiled. "The silencer, I mean. You must have hidden it before you came to get your father, since we did not find it on you. Still, if you had such a weapon, why would you resort to cutting poor Rodrigo's throat?"

"He pissed me off," she said.

"Apparently. However, I must ask if you came here alone."

"I don't see anybody else, do you?"

"Indeed not," Aguillar replied. And that was what worried him.

"Well, there you are."

"We'll talk more later," he assured her, "when you've had an opportunity to rest. Meanwhile, feel free to reminisce about old times."

"Fuck off."

"The family motto, I presume." Aguillar shook his head and turned back toward the door. "Americans. So brash, impetuous. So careless with their lives."

He placed two sentries on the prison hut this time: one at the door, the other standing watch in back. He didn't want to think that there were any other adversaries lurking in the woods, but he couldn't be sure. Until he had extracted further information from the woman, using any means available, he had to be on alert against the possibility of further raids. And that meant reinforcements, since they didn't have the vehicles available for swift evacuation of the camp.

His aide was waiting for him when he left the prison hut, and Aguillar began bombarding him with orders. "Fetch me Pablo Vega," he demanded. "And I want the sergeant of the guard to find out why his men saw nothing while the woman crept into our camp."

"Yes, sir."

"Do it now."

He let the anger power him back toward his quarters, through the first pale light of dawn. It couldn't be too late, he told himself. Failure was death.

And he was still too young to die.

12

She should have kept her mouth shut. Mercy Hastings cursed herself for letting the guerrilla leader trick her into speaking. Name, rank and serial number: that was the drill. She never should have let herself be suckered into goading him, thereby revealing information that she didn't even know she had.

"What's wrong?" her father asked, tuned in to Mercy's mood somehow, despite their general situation.

"I'm just thinking of a way to get us out of here," she lied.

That *was* a part of what was on her mind, but there was curiosity, as well. When she had found the solitary dead man, on the trail, she had assumed there was some trouble with his comrades, something that provoked them into killing him. It never crossed her mind that someone else was following the rebels, too, and whittling down their numbers in the dark.

Who could it be?

She flashed on Mike Belasko's somber face, and instantly recoiled.

"You've done the best you could," her father said. "I only wish that you were safe at home."

"I'm not done yet," she told him, straining at the rope that pinned her arms behind her back. His hands were bound, as well, the shackle reattached to a secure leg of the cot. Whatever Mercy did, she would be forced to do it for herself.

The bastards hadn't shackled her, at least, which gave her some mobility. She sat on the floor, rocked backward until her weight was on her shoulders, with her knees pulled up against her chest. It was a tight squeeze, but after three false starts, she stretched her arms enough to slip her feet between them, gasping with relief now that her hands were clasped in front of her.

"What are you doing, Mercy?"

"Shh!" She silenced him as if he were a pesky child, already reaching for the switchblade hidden in her sock. The men who searched her had been satisfied with turning out her pockets, fondling Mercy in the process, but they hadn't found the knife that she had liberated from the man she killed. She pressed the button on its handle, satisfied as the six-inch blade snapped into place. She tried the edge and found it razor-sharp.

"Your hands," she said, her father turning on command to let her saw the ropes apart. When he was free, she handed him the switchblade, pommel first, and said, "Now me."

"If they come back and find us—"

"Do it!" she commanded through clenched teeth.

He cut the rope that bound her wrists, and Mercy took the switchblade back before he had a chance to think of keeping it away from her.

"They'll kill you. Kill us both," he said.

"We're dead already if we don't get out of here."

"You won't be able to surprise them this time."

He was right, she thought, at least in terms of tackling the guard outside their door. As soon as Mercy turned the doorknob, he would shout a warning, maybe turn and fire on reflex. Either way, she was as good as dead.

"We still need guns," she said. "We'll have to wait until they come back. Meanwhile…"

She knelt and started on the wooden floor, to free the second cot, praying that the knife blade wouldn't snap and leave her to confront the enemy bare-handed.

"Jesus, Mercy!"

When she smiled, this time, there was a hard edge to it, and her words hit home with Garrick Hastings.

"Dad, you're *really* getting on my nerves, okay? So, if you don't have something nice to say, then don't say anything at all."

The next thing Mercy knew, her dad was chuckling to himself. It was infectious, and she had to bite her lip from laughing loud enough to bring the guards before she wanted them.

Not yet, she thought. She needed just ten more minutes, and a little luck.

And Mercy wondered if anyone was up there listening.

FOR REASONS best known to the planners of the camp, the radio equipment was located in a tent rather than in one of the more solid bungalows. The spike of its antenna guided Bolan to a point on the perimeter where he was less than ten yards distant from the west, or rear, wall of the tent. He drew his Ka-bar knife, glanced to left and right and braced himself before he made his move.

The sergeant of the guard had shaken up his men on the perimeter, since Mercy made her way into the camp and started raising hell. The troops on watch were walking beats now, rather than remaining stationary, but it made no difference in the long run. Bolan would be risking everything to cross that open stretch of ground, but there was no alternative.

He waited for the sentry on his section of the perimeter to pass and move downrange. When he was thirty-five or forty feet away, the Executioner rushed forward, slit the taut wall of the tent enough to make his way inside.

It was an all-out gamble, Bolan realized before he ever made the move. If there was someone in the tent, a warning cry or gunshot would bring the whole camp down on top of him, and that would be the end. In fact, the tent was empty, and he let his pent-up breath escape in a sigh of relief.

The radio wasn't the most sophisticated unit in the world, but it was powerful enough for him to reach an audience in Lima and beyond. It was attached to storage batteries, rechargeable, and while he hadn't used this brand before, the controls were both simple and self-explanatory. Moments after entering the tent, he had the unit humming, fiddling with the dials to find the proper frequency.

He knew which frequency was used by the security police in Lima from his talk with Captain Chavez, as a hedge against the possibility that Bolan might lack access to a telephone as he proceeded with his mission. Dialing up the proper numbers, he had to wonder who would be listening on the other end, and whether Chavez would receive the message Bolan had in mind. It was entirely possible, he realized, that someone opposed to the captain's aims would intercept the bulletin and pass it on to hostile hands, but he would have to take that chance. Likewise, if it was passed off as some kind of hoax and totally ignored, his effort would have been in vain.

Still, Bolan had to try. Before he made a one-man play against the numbers, risking Mercy and her father in what could turn out to be a bloody waste of time, he had to try enlisting aid from the security police. In that regard, for Bolan's purposes, it mattered little who responded to the call, as long as they turned out in force and made their presence felt without undue delay.

Because time mattered now. He felt it in his bones. If the Shining Path troops weren't interrogating Mercy and her father at the moment, they wouldn't postpone the questioning for long. It was too much for mere coincidence, the daughter of a hostage turning up at their remote retreat. Their leader had to be frantic now, attempting to divine who else might drop in to derail his best-laid plans.

Another possibility was that Mercy's interference might provoke the rebels into breaking camp before the uniforms arrived. In that case, Bolan would be forced to act alone. He couldn't let them leave with hostages, now that he had them in his sights.

He was about to start transmitting, when he heard the tent flap whisper at his back. Bolan swiveled on the wooden stool provided for the communications operator, reaching for the silenced 93-R in its shoulder rig. A young rebel stared at him, uncertain how he should react to stumbling on a gringo in the camp. He wore a pistol, but his time ran out before he started reaching for it, still too startled for a warning cry.

The gun in Bolan's hand coughed twice, both rounds on target, ripping through the man's chest. He staggered, dropping to his knees, and seemed about to gasp a warning, when the third round entered through his open lips and clipped his spinal column where it joined the skull. His lifeless body toppled forward, sprawling facedown in the dirt. Bolan waited, frozen with his pistol aiming at the entrance to the tent, in case the dead man had companions following behind him.

Forty seconds later, satisfied that no one else was on the way, he set the pistol near his right elbow, turning his full attention once more to the radio controls. His own pulse kept time with the doomsday numbers running in his head.

The Executioner and those he sought to save were swiftly running out of time.

THE MESSAGE REACHED Constantion Chavez at 9:13 a.m. A trusted aide approached his office cubicle, with sidelong glances toward the scattered uniforms who occupied the larger squad room. Nervous looking, obviously ill at ease, the young man offered an apology for interrupting Chavez at his work, then handed him a folded piece of paper torn off from a standard office memo pad. The message was succinct and chilling.

> To: Capt. C. Chavez, Eyes Only
> From: Belasko
>
> Major S.P. concentration found near Yauyos. Lat. approx. 12°2' S.; Long. approx. 76°1' W. Two hostages involved. Suggest proceed with all dispatch and care.
>
> MB

"You received this when?" Chavez demanded.

The young aide glanced at his wristwatch. "It has not yet been five minutes, Captain."

"All right." He found a piece of paper and began to write a list of twenty names, first making sure that there was nothing underneath to hold a clear impression of the words he wrote. When finished, Chavez passed the folded paper to his aide and said, "I want these officers assembled now without delay. No substitutions, no excuses. Do you understand?"

"Yes, sir."

"Have them draw field gear and the necessary weapons from supply, then meet me at the helipad in half an hour. Any questions?"

"No, sir."

Chavez knew he would have to call in some favors to get the helicopters he required, but he wasn't without influence. There had been a scandal, he recalled, involving the young daughter of Lieutenant Ricardo Ramirez, which Chavez had kept from both the press and the lieutenant's highly critical superiors. If no one else had signed out the helicopters, there should be no great difficulty in obtaining them for an unscheduled "practice exercise." And if Belasko's message was correct and Chavez managed to retrieve the American hostage while disrupting a substantial gathering of the Shining Path, no one would be too inclined to wonder how the "practice run" had turned into an all-out push against the enemy.

He had the bare bones of a story worked out in his mind—an aerial maneuver executed over open country, interrupted by the startling appearance of a rebel camp below—as he was reaching for the telephone to call Ramirez, presently the daytime officer in charge of maintenance on rolling stock and aircraft for the Lima headquarters of the security police. The story would need some refinement as he went along, adjusting for specific details that could neither be deleted or revised to fit a lie, but he would manage. Even if he wound up being chastised for his use of helicopters without prior approval from the brass, their outrage would be tempered by relief at finding Garrick Hastings still alive, plus any casualties inflicted on the Shining Path. As was the rule of most bureaucracies around the world, Chavez knew it was easier to win forgiveness than advance permission for a daring plan.

The telephone was answered after three rings at the other end. Chavez identified himself, asked for Ramirez, waiting thirty seconds for the middle-aged lieutenant to come on the line. When they were done with the routine of military courtesy, Chavez explained his need and waited through some twenty seconds of unhappy silence, smiling to himself as the lieutenant granted his request without an argument. Ramirez was a good man, and they understood each other.

He was on his way.

Much of the rest, he realized, came down to luck. If something went awry, and Chavez either missed the target or arrived too late to save the diplomat, then he couldn't expect much understanding from his own superiors. A total miss, with no contact, was one thing; he might get off with a simple reprimand for skipping proper channels when he signed the helicopters out. If his involvement led to Garrick Hastings's death, though, it would be another matter altogether. That could lead to revelation of his contact with Belasko, maybe even charges of complicity in a conspiracy against the state. If nothing else, his role in the extinction of a U.S. diplomat would finish any hope he had of rising further up the ladder of command in the security police.

Still, it was worth a try.

If he delayed—or, worse, ignored Belasko's message—then whatever happened to the hostage from that moment forward would be partly his fault. Worse, although the woman wouldn't count in an official reckoning, Chavez considered her predicament almost as much his fault as hers. If he, or persons under his command, had been more competent, the gringa would be on an airplane bound for the United States by now instead of sitting in a jungle camp somewhere, surrounded by bloodthirsty rebels.

It was his job to retrieve her, and to keep the promise he had made to Belasko. Even if it cost him dearly, Chavez was a man who kept his word, or gave his all in the attempt. If that meant putting his career and pension on the line to make up for an error by his own subordinates, so be it.

The opportunity to strike a telling blow at the Shining Path was a bonus, frosting on the cake.

As he replaced the telephone receiver in its cradle, Chavez wondered whether it was truly possible to have his cake and eat it, too.

MAJOR PADILLA DIDN'T fully understand the message his communication officer had managed to collect by accident, while he was monitoring traffic on the frequency reserved for use by the security police, but he was mightily intrigued. There was enough in it to whet his appetite and make him halt the general sweep that he had ordered, north of Yauyos, for his missing troops.

"Capt. C. Chavez" had to be his longtime adversary back at headquarters, although Padilla had no clue to the identity of this Belasko person who was sending out "Eyes Only" messages to Chavez from the countryside. The mention of two hostages was likewise puzzling, but Padilla rapidly dismissed it as irrelevant and concentrated on the geographical coordinates for a "Major S.P. concentration found near Yauyos."

Eagerly the major spread a large-scale map in front of him and found the reference point. Even allowing for the fact that the coordinates were said to be approximate, it was a better shot than wasting hours or days in fruitless marching through the forest. Even if he found his missing soldiers dead, as he had now resigned himself that they had to be, the task of tracking down their killers would still remain. But if he could jump that intervening step, eliminate the middleman, he had a chance to catch the rebels off their guard and punish them for their affront to civilized society.

A list of problems came to mind before his plan took

shape inside Padilla's head. The message might be false, for starters, a deliberate decoy meant for him or some informer lying to Chavez. Even assuming that the odds were fifty-fifty, though, Padilla couldn't well afford to shrug off the message.

Another problem was that it might prove to be a group of rebels other than the men who had—apparently—waylaid his officers. That posed no real deterrent to Padilla, since he didn't plan on taking any prisoners. There would be no one to dispute his version of events, no great incentive for the state to run ballistics tests between whatever guns he captured and the slugs extracted from his men, assuming they were ever found. In fact a sizable contingent of Shining Path rebels near the scene where loyal policemen had been lost was prima facie evidence of their involvement in the crime, and once their punishment had been inflicted in the field, Padilla handling any future evidence that was received by the police, there would be no one left to plead their case.

The final troubling note was the notation of "Two hostages involved." Padilla knew of only one man kidnapped by the Shining Path since April, and the odds of Garrick Hastings being found near Yauyos were no better than in any other town or village in Peru. The second hostage—if, in fact, a flesh-and-blood reality—would be a mystery until the smoke cleared on the battlefield and he had time to sort the pieces out.

It would be nice, Padilla thought, if he could find a way to free whatever hostages the traitors had secured, but he couldn't be held responsible for anything that happened once the raid began. No one other than himself and his communications officer would ever know he had received the message meant for Captain Chavez. He was simply searching for his missing officers, when he got lucky, struck the Shining Path encampment and proceeded to inflict the worst defeat those traitors had sustained in years. If innocent civilians got caught in the cross fire, that would be regrettable, of course, but no blame would attach to Serafin Padilla for the inadvertent tragedy.

And if worse came to worst, if it was all a hoax, Padilla would escape embarrassment by telling anyone who asked that he was simply looking for the men who vanished the previous night while on patrol. With luck he might even locate their bodies in the process to support his fabricated explanation of the coming raid.

It was a no-lose situation for Padilla, all except for one small point: now that he had a firm location for his adversaries, he couldn't leave the hunting to subordinates. Restricted to ground travel as he was, it wouldn't do for him to send the troops ahead, let them do all the fighting, while he tagged along behind with the photographers. Padilla wanted footage that would prove his own decisive role in the engagement, and that meant that he would have to hit the jungle trail.

"The things I do for God and country," he lamented to himself before he started shouting orders to his troops. "Five minutes, Captain! I want everyone prepared to go! No stragglers!"

"Yes, sir!"

As he strapped on his pistol, Padilla felt a strange mixture of apprehension and excitement. It was almost like the old days, when he had been rising through the ranks, but this was better.

This time he would leave the killing to his men.

And claim the glory for himself.

RECEPTION OF THE MESSAGE was confirmed, and Bolan switched the set off, picked up his Beretta and returned it to its armpit holster. Whether Chavez got the message, or would act on it, was anybody's guess. The Executioner had played his only card in terms of bringing reinforcements to his aid, and he would simply have to wait it out as long as possible.

But first he had to get out of camp.

And take the dead man with him.

Another corpse would turn the camp into a seething anthill. There was no way they could blame the second death on Mercy Hastings, and the implications of a radio transmission to the outside world were obvious. If anything could spook the rebels into bailing out before the cavalry arrived, that ought to do it, and his task was now to keep them stationary for as long as possible, unless he sensed some mortal danger to the hostages.

The first job, Bolan knew, was to clean up his mess. The dead man lying at his feet was leaking crimson from his mouth and two chest wounds, the impact of the head shot having been absorbed by skull and vertebrae. It was a simple thing to roll him over on his back, and so arrest the flow of blood, while Bolan scuffed the dirt floor of the tent in an attempt to hide the rusty-colored stains. He couldn't do a perfect job without a rake or hoe, but it was good enough to pass a superficial scan by someone who wasn't expecting evidence of homicide.

Bolan slit the dead man's shirttail with the Ka-bar knife, cutting strips that he stuffed into the bloody mouth and chest wounds, damming the flow of blood from veins and arteries that had no pulse to empty them. That done, he double-checked the tent, scooped up the cartridge casings he had spent and put them in his pocket.

Done.

The long slit in the tent's west wall was hopeless, but it hadn't drawn attention yet, and he would need it for his getaway. He left the rebel's body where it was and took a cautious peek outside, checking the nearest guard, how close he was and how long it would take for him to pass.

When he was finished with his calculations, Bolan picked up the corpse and balanced it across one shoulder in the classic fireman's carry, with the Steyr and Uzi dangling on their shoulder straps, the 93-R cocked and ready in his hand.

Split-second timing was required to pull this off, and if he failed, it would well and truly hit the fan. He had no doubt of his ability to take out one sentry, but even if the rebel made no noise in dying, Bolan would be back to the original dilemma of an extra corpse in camp and its inevitable impact on the other terrorists. Escaping with his own skin in one piece was less important to him, at the moment, than preserving the illusion of normality among his enemies, while he was waiting for Chavez and his relief contingent to arrive.

He heard the sentry pass and glimpsed movement through the narrow slit his blade had opened in the canvas, waiting long enough to let the gunman put some ground between them. Slipping through the makeshift exit, Bolan almost lost it when his lifeless passenger got stuck, one of his boots snagged on the canvas, but he tugged it free without enough noise to disturb the sentry, who was walking with his back turned less than fifty feet away.

From there, it was a short dash to the tree line, running in a crouch and praying that he hadn't missed a second lookout somewhere on the camp's perimeter. There were no shots or shouted warnings as he slipped into the forest, traveling another fifty yards before he dared to stop and place his burden against a tree trunk.

He needed height to keep watch on the prison hut and make sure Mercy Hastings and her father weren't moved. Pure logic told him that the officer in charge of the facility, whoever that turned out to be, would seek more answers from the woman in short order, but if she was thought to be alone, the inquisition might have just a tad less urgency. Whatever time he gained from that point on, it was a point for his side, bringing Captain Chavez that much closer to the target zone.

Or maybe not.

Bolan was fairly confident in his ability to judge a man on short acquaintance, but he also knew that there were many factors outside his control that could delay Chavez or totally prevent him from responding to the call for help. Worst case, the message could have been diverted, kept from Chavez altogether. There were also various logistical problems to consider: transportation, mustering the troops, evading sticky questions from the brass when he was ready to depart. It never once occurred to Bolan that Chavez would get the message and refuse to come, but willingness and capability were often very different things.

If Chavez didn't come, if no one came, then he would do the job himself to the best of his ability. He had the charges in the motor pool and enough hardware to raise some hell among the terrorists. It still might work.

But Bolan didn't care to bet his life and two civilian hostages on sucker odds if there was any other way to go.

He moved back toward the camp, picked out his tree and climbed up. When he had found a perch that let him cover all the vital players, he leaned back against the trunk and settled in to wait.

13

The stranger's blood had dried on Mercy's hands while they were bound behind her back. She rubbed them briskly while she waited, shedding flakes of rusty brown that scattered on the wooden floor like grains of cinnamon. She found her father watching when she glanced up, and the grin she faked would never be mistaken for an honest smile.

"I wish you hadn't come," he said.

"I had no choice."

"For heaven's sake—"

"Don't start, okay? We don't have time. You want to chew me out for caring, it will have to wait."

"I'm sorry, hon," he said. "I'm scared for you, that's all."

"I'm scared for both of us. What we need to do is concentrate on getting out of here as soon as possible."

"There are too many of them," he insisted.

"If you start to think that way, then one's too many. Who's the soldier here?"

"You are," he answered, managing the bare suggestion of a smile.

"All right, then. Just because they spotted us the first time, doesn't mean we're out of luck. They aren't expecting any trouble while we're hog-tied. Is the chain okay?"

He raised his leg, where she had wrapped the shackle

snug around his calf once more. "I'll manage if we get that far," he said.

"The arm?"

"I'm fine. But I don't much like our prospects in the daylight without guns."

"They're sitting down to breakfast," Mercy said, her nostrils twitching at the smell of food. "And we'll have guns. Don't worry. Just do what I told you, when I make my move."

"All right."

Her father didn't sound convinced, but Mercy reckoned he would do his part when it was time. He didn't have much choice, in fact, if he intended to survive.

She had finally convinced him that the guerrillas didn't mean to let them go. It was a simple exercise in logic— no one bothering to hide his face around the captives, freely using names, no evident negotiations with the world outside. She was a bit surprised to find her father still alive, concluding that the terrorists were saving him for some special occasion, when his death, presumably, would have more impact on their enemies. She didn't need to know the details. Every moment spent among their captors shaved the odds in favor of survival, urging her to hurry.

The muffled sound of voices on the doorstep warned her that their time was coming. Mercy sat up, with her ankles pressed together, hands behind her back, the open switchblade clutched in her right fist. The door swung open and a bearded man entered, regarding them with evident disinterest, carrying a metal plate of food in either hand. Behind him, standing back a pace or two, their watchdog kept his eyes fixed on the doorway, more concerned with what was happening outside than with his prisoners.

The hardman was staring at them, wondering how they

could eat the meager breakfast with their hands tied. He wasn't about to feed them, and he asked the sentry for permission to untie their bonds. The lookout shrugged, and the bearded man bent to place the two plates on the floor.

He went to Mercy first, a smug grin on his face, bent close enough for her to smell his garlic breath and told her, "Turn around."

She whipped the knife around and drove it underneath his chin, the whiskers tickling her hand. A rapid sawing motion, and a fresh cascade of crimson spattered her. She was already moving as the dying man slumped forward, gasping silently, his voice box ruined by the stroke that severed his carotid artery. Behind her Mercy heard her father grappling for the soldier's pistol, but her eyes and mind were focused on the rifleman in front of her, just turning to confront an unexpected threat.

Her elbow caught him in the throat, momentum slamming him against the nearest wall, as Mercy drove a knee into his crotch. The switchblade entered just above his navel, ripping upward, drenching her with blood before it found his heart. If he had kept his finger on the trigger of his M-16, the gunner might have managed to alert his comrades with a warning shot, but it was too late now. His legs turned into rubber, buckling at the knees, and Mercy eased his lifeless body to the floor.

She took the rifle from him, found its safety still engaged and hastily corrected the mistake. Another moment, and his bloodstained bandolier was looped around her own neck, spare mags resting heavily across her breasts. She turned to find her father buckling on the first man's pistol belt.

"They say third time's the charm," she told him, "but I don't believe we'll get another chance if we blow this one."

"So," he said, "I guess we'd better get it right."

"I'd say."

"I'm glad I've got a soldier here to help me out."

"We'd better do it, then."

"Hey, listen…just in case I haven't said it recently…"

"I know," she said. "I love you, too." She smiled briefly before she said, "Now, can we go?"

HE RECKONED there was trouble when the two men didn't reappear immediately from the prison hut, but Bolan told himself it could be anything—some kind of argument, maybe the extra time it took releasing bonds, so Mercy and her father could consume the breakfast one of the terrorists was carrying. It could be anything, he thought, and kept that optimistic point of view in mind for all of thirty seconds more—until he saw Mercy peek out through the open doorway.

He had to give her credit for persistence in the face of overwhelming odds, but that could just as easily get Mercy Hastings and her father killed as win their freedom. Bolan cursed and scrambled down the tree trunk.

He hit the turf in a crouch and whipped the Steyr free of its shoulder sling, thumbing off the safety as he broke toward the perimeter of the encampment. Bolan had no plan in mind, the game was moving much too fast for a coherent strategy, but he knew Mercy and her father would need some cover if the rebels spotted them. And how could they avoid it in broad daylight, with the camp on full alert?

The shooting started seconds later, one short burst from a Kalashnikov to start the party, its distinctive rattle readily identifiable to anyone who had once been on the receiving end. A pistol cracked in answer—or, perhaps, in concert—with the automatic rifle, then a submachine gun opened up, and it all went to hell from there.

He did the first thing he could think of, reaching for the detonator on his belt and arming it while he was on the move, his thumb mashing the button down a heartbeat later. Sudden thunder rocked the compound as the motor pool went up in smoke and flames, the clustered vehicles erupting like a string of giant fireworks as the charges blew.

The motor pool was situated on the far side of the compound from the prison hut, and Bolan had no fear of Mercy or her father catching any shrapnel from the blast. With any luck at all, it would provide an adequate diversion for the hostages, to let them reach the tree line while their adversaries were distracted, ducking chunks of red-hot steel and trying to discover what was happening.

He didn't dwell on the alternative. Failure was unacceptable to Bolan's mind, but altogether possible whenever human beings were involved. Still running, he reached back for his fanny pack and drew a 40 mm rifle grenade, fitting it to the factory-standard launcher on his Steyr AUG. Before he reached the camp's perimeter, the HE round was ready, primed to fly. All Bolan needed was a target, and he found it in the mess tent, where at least two dozen rebels were collected, fumbling with their guns and gaping at the flaming ruins of the motor pool.

The camp stove was an older butane model, standing off to one side of the mess tent, to the left of the assembled troops. He brought the rifle to his shoulder, sighted quickly and squeezed off before he had a chance to hesitate. The Steyr bucked against his shoulder, and the 40 mm round went hurtling toward its target, stabilized by stubby tail fins.

It was loaded with an impact fuse that detonated when it struck the camp stove's butane tank. A fireball wrapped itself around the two men standing closest to the stove and sent them lurching from the tent, arms flapping, trailing wings of flame.

He let them run and swiveled toward the others, caught between two nightmares now. The shock wave from the closer blast had knocked a couple of them down, but they were struggling to their feet and groping for the weapons they had dropped, the others raising guns and looking for a target as the Executioner unleashed a stream of lead that swept them from left to right, chest high.

He didn't wait to judge the impact of his fusillade, withdrawing instantly and following the tree line toward the hut where Mercy and her father had been held. The riflefire had sputtered out in that direction, but that didn't mean the two of them were safe, by any means. They had been seen, and someone would be after them as soon as the guerrillas could recover from their triple shock.

And that wouldn't take long, if they were any kind of soldiers.

Bolan saw the prison hut ahead of him and to his right. He looked for Mercy and her father, and caught a glimpse of movement in the trees, some thirty yards away, blue denim slipping into shadow. Bolan palmed another grenade, with four remaining in the fanny pack, and mounted it as three guerrillas closed in toward the hut.

This one was easy, firing from the hip, with no need to aim. The hut exploded, flinging jagged shards of plywood all around, the metal roof pitched skyward on a tongue of flame, then settling back to earth. The gunners nearest to the blast were flung to earth, but they staggered to their feet a moment later, shaking off the dust, unharmed. Instead of dropping them, and thereby drawing more attention to himself, the Executioner retreated through the trees.

An organized pursuit wouldn't be long in coming, he realized, and he would have to overtake the fugitives before their enemies could do so, try to help them out somehow without allowing either one of them to shoot him in the process.

He turned his back on the chaotic camp and got a fix on the location where he had glimpsed Mercy Hastings moments earlier. There was no sign of her by now, of course, but he would pick up traces on the way. The runners had no time to hide their tracks, and while that worked to Bolan's benefit, it would likewise assist the hunting party coming after him.

So little time, and he could feel his plan unraveling around him, but he had to play the cards as they were dealt to him. A front-line soldier rarely got to pick the game, but he could always name the stakes.

For they were always life and death.

IT FELT AS IF he had been running for an hour or more, but Garrick Hastings knew that only moments had elapsed since their escape. He tried to keep himself in shape with twice-weekly workouts at the gym, but nothing had prepared him for this mad dash through the forest, running for his life.

The altitude and rough terrain contributed significantly to his near exhaustion, Hastings realized, but there was also fear, approaching panic since the moment he had stepped outside the hut and known that he could die at any moment—worse, that he might see his daughter killed, before the bullets cut him down. She was his only family, these days, not quite the living image of his wife, but close enough that seeing Mercy die would be a double shock.

It was the thought of losing her, more than an impulse to protect himself, that made him fire the pistol he had lifted from the dead man in the prison hut. When he saw rebels pointing toward them, moving rapidly in their direction, and his daughter had unleashed a burst of automatic fire to slow them, Hastings had raised the handgun, squeezing off two rounds without a second thought. He had no reason to believe that he had killed or wounded anyone, but it was still a shock, when he had time to think about it afterward, as they were racing through the trees.

So *this* was what it felt like in a war. He had been draft-deferred for college, during Vietnam, and thankful for it. Later, after graduation, they had changed the rating system and eliminated call-ups, part of Nixon's bid to win a second term. It couldn't save his lying ass from Watergate, but Garrick Hastings had been pleased to take advantage of the change in rules that let him off the hook. And it had never crossed his mind, in all the years since then, that he would ever have to kill a man, much less run from a pack of Communist guerrillas through a godforsaken jungle, several thousand miles from home.

He was fading fast, lungs burning, the muscles in his thighs and calves already spiked with pain that would explode as full-blown cramps before he went much farther. Mercy was in better shape, and trained for a run like this, he realized. She might escape if she were on her own, but not with him to hold her back. Yet if he suggested separating, she would never buy it. She was too damned smart for him to pull the wool over her eyes. She had her mother's second sight that way.

It had been stunning, back there in the camp, when he had watched her kill three men before his very eyes. It was bizarre, this new glimpse of his daughter. Even knowing that the Army had to have trained her for this kind of situation, teaching her to kill, his mind had never drawn the obvious connection. He had seen his little girl in uniform, some half a dozen times, but she was never armed on those occasions, and he never really thought of her in combat, where she would have to kill without remorse.

My hands are wet. Her first words came back to him, when she had found him in the rebel camp, blood crimson bright on Mercy's palms and fingers, from the first man she had killed.

He didn't have that kind of courage, Hastings realized. When he was shooting at the enemy back there, it was a reflex action, more for Mercy than himself. To creep up on a man from hiding, with a knife and slit his throat, that kind of killing took more than instruction. It required a certain mind-set, grim determination, an ability to separate yourself from "normal" human feelings while you carried out the act—and afterward, as well.

What other changes had he missed in Mercy, Hastings wondered, since they parted company three years ago? In spite of everything a father always hoped, he knew that she was probably no virgin, and the mental images *that* thought evoked were ten times worse than any mortal combat. There had been a time, not all that long ago, when Hastings had believed that she would always be his little girl. A part of him still thought of her that way—or had, until she stepped into the prison hut with bloody hands and proved how very wrong he was.

He was completely baffled by the racket of explosions and more gunfire coming from the camp. Mercy hadn't looked back, except to check on him from time to time, and Hastings wondered if she knew what kind of hell was breaking loose back there. How could she? If there had been time for her to rig explosives in the compound, surely Mercy would have mentioned it while they were tied up in the hut.

What, then?

Perhaps one of their bullets had been lucky, setting off the fuel tank of a rebel vehicle or striking sparks inside their ammo cache, but Hastings didn't think so. Such a fluke might possibly account for one explosion, but the other two had been delayed by several moments, long enough for him to follow Mercy better than a hundred yards from the camp. And accidental blasts wouldn't account for further gunfire, after they were out of sight.

He drew another blank and gave it up, as tangled roots reached out to trip him, almost bringing him to hands and knees. He caught himself, flayed one palm in the process, but he hardly felt the burning pain. His total life experience boiled down to lungs, legs and the pounding in his skull that told him he was close to passing out.

If he lost it, fell along the way, he knew that Mercy would remain beside him until hope was gone, the enemy surrounding her. And she would fight before she let the two of them be caged again.

Which meant that she would die.

He couldn't let that happen. Hastings focused on his breathing, hoping he could beat the strain and altitude if he tried hard enough. Long-distance runners did it all the time, small consolation, in itself, but something he could shoot for, grasping like a drowning man who saw a twig above him, floating on the surface, and imagined it to be a giant log.

He hadn't run this long or hard since the high-school track team, and in those days his incentive had been glory, something to impress the girls and his coach. There was no life-or-death about it in the good old days. That had to wait until his muscles, heart and lungs were pushing fifty, too much life behind him for his body to perform as if he were a boy, still full of piss and vinegar.

But he would run until he dropped, for Mercy's sake. And when that happened, if he still had strength enough to lift the stolen pistol, he would fight for her until he died.

He owed her that much, anyway.

It was the very least that he could do.

IT WAS NO TRICK to overtake the fugitives. Mercy was quick and had a fair sense of direction, but her father slowed her. Within a quarter of an hour, Bolan had located them and moved some forty yards ahead, unnoticed by his quarry. He was waiting for them when they reached a rushing mountain stream and started looking for a way across.

"You need to stop and think it through," he said from out of nowhere.

Mercy spun to face the sound of Bolan's voice, but held her fire. Her father looked confused, but held a pistol ready in his hand.

"Belasko?"

"In the flesh," Bolan said, stepping into the open from behind a sturdy tree.

"You followed me?" He couldn't tell if it was anger or amazement in her voice.

"I thought you were in Lima," Bolan stated, "until you walked into the camp and gave yourself away."

"I'll *bet* you thought I was in Lima." There was no mistaking Mercy's anger now. "You set me up with the security police."

"I take it you two know each other," Garrick Hastings said.

"We've met," his daughter snapped. "Once was enough."

"From where I stand, you need some help right now."

"We're all right," Mercy answered, but she was clearly bluffing now, her heart not in it.

"What I would suggest," the Executioner went on, ignoring her bravado, "is that you get across that stream and head due west, another five, six miles. You'll strike what passes for a highway in this neighborhood. Keep on northwest from there until you reach the nearest town.

They'll have a telephone or shortwave radio, and you can touch base with the embassy. Take this."

He tossed the compass, watching as Mercy caught it with her left hand.

"What about you?" she asked reluctantly.

"I'm not done here."

"You blew the camp?"

"I gave you a diversion. No big deal. They have a lesson coming."

Mercy saw where he was going with it. "I should stay."

"That's negative. You came to help your father out. Mission accomplished, soldier. Take it home."

"We...I can't just leave you here," she said.

"I'd be here if you hadn't come along," he told her. "Only, then, your father wouldn't have safe conduct back to Lima. Don't confuse your job with mine."

"You said—"

"There's been a change of plan," he interrupted her. "And right now you're wasting precious time."

"All right, then, dammit! Dad, let's go!"

"You'll find it easier to cross about a hundred yards upstream."

They left without another word, though Garrick Hastings hesitated long enough to raise a hand in parting. Then he followed Mercy up the gentle slope until they disappeared among the trees.

Bolan left them to it, turning his mind at once to the defensive preparations for his stand. The fugitives had left a trail that any woodsman worth his salt could follow in the dark, much less broad daylight, and the trackers would be coming soon.

The Executioner was counting on it.

He prepared himself by seeking cover. The roost he chose would let him overlook the rugged ground that led back toward the rebel camp and spot the trackers coming from a range of forty yards or so. They might be audible before he saw them, but the field of fire was adequate to let him stop them, even if they took him by surprise.

Another seven minutes, and he heard them coming through the trees. They didn't speak to one another, but they weren't stealthy, either, counting on the fact that their intended prey would run all out until exhaustion brought them down. The first priority was catching up, to make the kill.

But none of them had reckoned on the Executioner.

He primed the Steyr with a 40 mm grenade and waited, aiming in the general direction of the noise. When he made target acquisition moments later, Bolan started counting heads. He came up with seven men, and figured he could handle it, even with room for error on the count.

Two pointmen led, and he found his mark between them, sighting on a boulder jutting from the earth. The range was thirty yards, and Bolan ducked back after firing, trusting the impact fuse to do its job.

The shock wave ruffled leaves above his head and brought a straggling burst of fire from those below. He rolled to his left and came up shooting, spotting one of them in the open, charging up the hill, all knees and elbows, slamming him back down the slope with half a dozen rounds.

One of the targets from his first shot lay unmoving, crumpled in a heap, while his companion moaned and wriggled in the weeds a few yards distant. Bolan looked for gunners on their feet and found two scurrying for cover on his right. He led the pointman, squeezing off a burst that seemed to jerk the runner's legs from under him and drop him on his face.

The second man in line leaped over his companion, diving for the cover of a fallen tree. He got there well ahead of Bolan's raking burst and burrowed in, prepared to make a stand. The Executioner unclipped a hand grenade and pulled the pin, checking left and right for hostile guns before he cocked his arm and made the pitch. It wobbled slightly in midair, but he was dead on target, watching it bounce once before it disappeared behind the log.

His adversary leaped erect and tried to run, but he was out of time. The blast gave him momentum, but he was ventilated by the shrapnel storm, stone dead before he hit the turf.

And that left two.

They could have cut and run, but they were macho men, determined not to shame themselves before a stranger. They attacked from different sides, as if on some unspoken signal, AK-47s hammering away at Bolan as they charged.

The shooter on his left was somewhat closer, thus a greater threat, and Bolan took him first, a roll-out to the left that allowed him to meet his adversary with a rising burst from twenty feet away. The bullets stopped him cold and spun him like a top, blood spouting from a dozen wounds as he went down.

The Steyr's bolt locked open on an empty chamber, and Bolan knew there was no time to reload, with angry hornets buzzing overhead and his would-be killer closing in a rush. He dropped the AUG and swung the silenced Uzi into line, flicking off the safety as he raised the SMG one-handed and sighted down the barrel as if it were an extraheavy pistol, holding down the trigger.

Bolan's adversary ran into a storm of parabellum manglers, the bullets jolting him off stride so that he tottered, reeling, and dropped backward on his haunches. Still, the AK-47 stuttered, pointed at the sky now, emptying its magazine before the gunman slumped back into silent, smoky death.

Grim silence fell across the killing ground. Downrange the second victim of his MECAR round lay still, no longer wriggling like a grounded trout. A smell of sudden death and gun smoke lingered on the air, resisting the first efforts of a gentle mountain breeze. He spent another moment with the dead, reloading weapons, counting his grenades.

He had a fair hike back to the guerrilla camp, but Bolan didn't mind. There should be ample time before the main event.

From where he stood, it would be downhill all the way.

14

They found a place to rest ten minutes after the reports of gunfire died away behind them. Garrick Hastings still kept listening for any noises of pursuit, but he was calming a bit, his pulse more regular.

"He stopped them," Mercy said.

"How can you tell?"

"Call it a hunch."

The tenor of her voice made Hastings frown. "Who was he?"

"*Is*, not *was*," she said. "They won't get rid of him that easily."

"All right, who *is* he, then?"

"Mike Belasko. I already told you that. We met in Lima."

She was holding something back; that much was obvious. The trick, Hastings thought, was to skirt the problem area and concentrate on basic facts.

"I mean, who is he? What is he?"

"I couldn't tell you," she replied, gaze drifting back in the direction they had come from, where the woods were deathly quiet now. "Some kind of soldier, covert style."

"And he was sent to find me?"

"So he said. I think it's obvious he had some other fish to fry while he was in the neighborhood."

"Mercy…"

"Don't start, okay? I know it was a dumb move, going

AWOL, coming down here on my own," she said, "but there was no way I could leave you hanging with a bunch of heartless bastards who care more about their public image than your life."

"I was about to thank you," Hastings said, "for everything."

"Oh. Well." Her voice was smaller, almost childlike.

"You showed courage," Hastings told his daughter. "More than I have, incidentally. The things you've done...the risks..."

His voice dried up just as his eyes began to water, and he turned away from Mercy, made a show of studying the trees, half wishing someone would emerge to challenge them, to let him prove himself.

It wasn't being rescued by a woman that embarrassed Hastings now, but rather being so dependent on a person he had previously regarded as a child. *His* child. Some parents never saw their children as adults, no matter what they did in life. It was a kind of mental block that came with parenthood and sometimes led to breakdowns in communication, even the disintegration of a family. Hastings knew that he had reacted to his wife's death by attempting to keep Mercy close, safe in his shadow, relegated to a mental never-never land where she would never age past sweet sixteen. He thought about the arguments his own behavior had provoked, the wedge it drove between them, sending Mercy off to join the military in an act of protest, burdened with a need to prove herself.

He grieved for so much wasted time.

"I'm sorry," Hastings said.

"For what?"

"A lot of things."

"You'll have to tell me later, then," she said. "It's time to move."

"Shouldn't we wait for him?"

Already on her feet, she glanced back at the trees and said, "He won't be coming, Dad. He went back for the others."

"Others?"

"The guerrillas."

"Why?"

"Why do you think?"

"One man? What can he do?"

"You'd be surprised," she said, and started moving to the west once more, a quick glance at the compass to confirm directions.

Hastings fell in step behind her, wondering what kind of man it was who faced several dozen gunmen on his own, who sent him, how much he was paid or whether money even entered into it. An obvious professional, Belasko still cared less about himself than helping others, finishing the job he had been sent to do.

And that thought raised more questions in itself. What *was* his job, exactly? Did the State Department know that he was down here, stalking soldiers of the Shining Path and flaunting half a dozen federal statutes in the process? Did the White House know?

Hastings had wondered how his old friend in the Oval Office would react to his abduction, knowing that the President of the United States—apparently all-powerful, to some—didn't have the unlimited authority to act as he saw fit, no matter whose life might be riding on the line.

Still…

Garrick Hastings made a mental note to check it out by any means available once he was safely back in the United States.

Meanwhile he kept the stolen pistol close at hand and followed in the footsteps of the woman who had been his child.

THE TRUCKS COULD ONLY take them so far north of Yauyos, after which most of the troopers had to disembark and walk. Major Padilla, riding in his jeep like any good commander, cursed the tight-fisted government that vetoed funds for building and maintaining rural highways, thereby slowing progress to a crawl. It wouldn't be the first time his pursuit of traitors had been hampered by terrain and transportation difficulties, nor did he suspect that it would be the last.

But another forty minutes ought to put them at the map coordinates dictated in the cryptic message to Chavez. If there was any substance to the warning, they should locate signs of human habitation even sooner: tracks and litter, early-warning sentries who would have to be eliminated. On the other hand, if it was all a wild-goose chase, then he was simply wasting time and energy.

Whichever way it went, Padilla vowed that he would have it out with Chavez first thing, when he got back to their headquarters in Lima. He would find out who or what "Belasko" was, and jerk the captain's chain for any breach of regulations he could document. If it was serious enough—or could be made to seem so, through manipulation of the facts—he might be able to remove Chavez entirely from the force, or even clap him into jail. That would be sweet, to see his rival stripped of rank and honor, locked up in a cage, conveyed to regular "debriefing" sessions with the most adept interrogators on Padilla's staff.

His smile was fleeting, lost when yet another pothole jarred the jeep and snapped his teeth together. Turning on the sergeant who had drawn a short straw to become his driver for the month, Padilla thundered, "Watch the road, for Christ's sake!"

"Yes, sir. I'm very sorry."

Sorry, be damned, Padilla thought. A road like this

could wreck a man. He turned and looked back at his troopers, marching doggedly behind the jeep, their only break the fact that frequent showers kept the road from being dry enough to issue choking dust.

The submachine gun in his lap was an "obsolete" American model, the 9 mm Smith & Wesson M-76, complete with folding stock and ventilated barrel shroud, with thirty-six rounds in the magazine. Padilla wasn't taking any chances this time out, not when they could be closing on a major group of Shining Path guerrillas. He wasn't afraid to fight, but it had been some time since he was on the firing line. The skills remained, but long inaction played hell with the nerves.

He would be fine, Padilla thought, once he could see the enemy. It was uncertainty and doubt that made him nervous, wondering if he had traveled all this way for nothing, just to lose his soldiers in the wilderness, while their assassins slipped away. The message he had intercepted could be false—or worse, he could be bait, designed to land the nearest group of soldiers or policemen in a lethal trap.

Padilla kept his eyes in constant motion, checking out the trees around him, probing shadows, waiting for the enemy to show himself. His losses were already heavy, but the mission could be turned around, transformed from a disaster to a triumph if he kept his wits about him, dodged the snares ahead and managed to inflict more damage on the enemy. If necessary, he could always boost the body count in his report to headquarters, but only if he made it back to Lima in one piece.

Winners wrote history. The losers—those who managed to survive—were relegated to a whining chorus that no one really heard or heeded. Serafin Padilla had his mind made up that he would be a winner, and that history would list this day as a resounding triumph for himself, his country and the rule of law.

Another pothole snapped Padilla from his reverie and made him curse the cringing driver. "How much farther?" he demanded.

"Two kilometers, Chief. Perhaps a little less."

Padilla checked his submachine gun, making sure it had a live round in the firing chamber, and switched off the safety.

Soon, he told himself. The enemy would feel his righteous anger soon.

ALONZO AGUILLAR SURVEYED the wreckage of his mountain camp with sullen fury burning in his heart. The motor pool and mess tent were destroyed, and leaping flames had seared the camou netting overhead, until it sagged and hung in blackened tatters. With eleven soldiers dead and thirteen wounded, his effective strength had been reduced by almost thirty-five percent. Another seven men had been dispatched to find the hostages and bring them back, alive or dead, but Aguillar couldn't be sure those men would ever make it back to camp.

His first instinct was to evacuate, before some fresh disaster struck, but it wasn't that simple. Without vehicles, his men would have to march on foot and carry all their gear, as well as the wounded. That meant choosing what equipment he would leave behind, which weapons he would sacrifice and how to best make sure they would be useless to his enemies. The latter problem could be solved with an explosive charge, but detonation of a bomb would only help to pinpoint their location, if the army or security police were prowling the area.

It troubled Aguillar that he couldn't pinpoint the moment when he lost control. Things had been bad in Lima when he left, but the retreat to Yauyos should have solved that problem. On the contrary, however, he was barely settled in when the young gringa came to fetch her father, like the gung-ho hero of some action movie in the States. Before he could determine how she found the camp, much less slipped past his guards and murdered one of them, the woman *and* his premier hostage had escaped, inflicting further damage in the process.

But they weren't alone.

Aguillar had been questioning survivors since the shooting stopped, and he was now convinced that some-one else had helped the pair escape. There was an outside chance the woman could have planted charges in the mo-tor pool before she was discovered, even one chance in a million that his soldiers could have missed a detonator when they searched her after she was caught. But all agreed the blast that took the mess tent out, immediately followed by another to the prison hut, had been produced by rockets of some kind. The woman definitely did *not* have that kind of hardware hidden on her person, nor had there been any time for her to raid the compound's armory and grab an RPG before she fled. Likewise, three survi-vors of the breakout had reported automatic-weapons fire from the perimeter, some fifty yards southwest of where the woman and her father disappeared into the trees.

That had to mean at least one other gunman firing on the camp, and maybe more than one. It also meant that Aguillar couldn't be certain all his enemies were gone. Some could be watching him that very moment, peering from the tree line, maybe staring at him through the cros-shairs of a telescopic rifle sight.

The very notion sent a shiver down his spine, but Aguillar refused to run and hide, behaving like a coward in the presence of his men. A shout from the direction of the communications tent drew him in that direction, trailed by half a dozen riflemen. He found one of his soldiers standing at a corner of the tent and pointing toward the back wall, where a long vertical slit had been cut in the canvas.

"Where is Pablo Vega?" Aguillar demanded. No one answered, the soldiers shifting nervously beneath his gaze until he shouted, "Find him! Bring him here to me!"

Three of the men ran off in different directions, calling Vega's name, but Aguillar wasn't entirely sure that they would find him. Something strange and sinister had happened here.

He stepped inside the tent and sniffed the air. Was that a hint of gun smoke? How could he be certain, when the reek of it was strong outside?

He crossed the tent and checked the radio. It was undamaged, but he didn't recognize the frequency selected on the tuner. When he switched it on, the voice of static whispered in his ears. Aguillar switched it off again and turned to scan the bare dirt floor. It had been scuffed, as if by heavy boots, but that wasn't suspicious in itself.

He knelt and used his fingernail to scratch a small stain in the dirt. It came off rusty brown, with no smell he could distinguish, when he raised the finger to his nostrils.

Blood? If so, what did it mean?

If Vega had been frightened by the gunfire and explosions in the compound, scared enough to run away, there would have been no one to stop him. Cutting through the back wall of the tent would be a useless bit of melodrama in the circumstances, for a soldier bailing out.

But not, Aguillar thought, for someone sneaking *in*.

The chill was back, but it didn't assist him in deciding what some unknown enemy would hope to find, in the tent. Since he, or they, hadn't destroyed the radio, it stood to reason he—or they—had hoped to send a message.

But what message? And to whom?

A sudden thought struck Aguillar with all the impact

of a punch between the eyes. He stiffened, turned back toward the radio and considered it in silence for a moment, then he bolted from the tent.

"We must evacuate!" he told the soldiers waiting for him, just outside. "There is no time to lose."

"But—"

"Now!" he snapped. "Collect the soldiers who can walk. Have each man take two extra rifles or one RPG, plus all the ammunition they can carry."

"And the wounded?" one man asked him.

"Never mind. Just do as you are told. I'll deal with them myself."

CONSTANTION CHAVEZ wasn't afraid of flying, but an open helicopter always made him edgy. Even belted in and seated well back from the open hatch, he had a childish fear that something would go wrong: the whirlybird would tip, his belt would come unbuckled—maybe rip free of the bolts that held it fast at either end—and he would plunge headlong through empty air to splatter on the ground a thousand feet below.

In fact, the captain realized, his greatest danger waited for him on the ground, where they were going. If Belasko's message was correct, a major concentration of guerrillas waited for him north of Yauyos, and Padilla's troops were also in the region, doing who knew what. It was a recipe for bloody chaos, but Chavez hadn't been able to refuse the invitation. He was bound to do his best and see what happened next.

Surprise would be his one advantage if his soldiers were outnumbered by the enemy. At that, while airborne strikes allowed for greater speed, mobility and impact, the security police didn't possess aircraft with any kind of stealth technology. The men he hunted would inevitably hear the choppers coming, but they might be lulled into believing it was just a flight in transit, heading somewhere else, until the final moment came, when it would be too late for them to run.

The flip side could be grim disaster. Chavez knew that some of the guerrilla bands had rocket launchers, .50-caliber machine guns captured from the military, all the hardware needed to destroy a helicopter in the air or bring it plummeting to earth in smoke and flames. There was a chance his men would never even get to fight on solid ground if they were spotted from the trees and targeted by weapons that could bring them down.

It troubled him to think of that, and so he concentrated on Belasko, wondering exactly what the American had found. He had been looking for the American hostage back in Lima, and Chavez could only speculate on what had taken him so far afield. If Garrick Hastings was among the rebels camped near Yauyos, then Chavez would have to use great caution to avoid endangering his life.

But how could he be sure? How would he ever know?

It was a problem not worth dwelling on at this point in the game. He had advised his soldiers that there might be gringos present, and that nothing should be done to harm them, if that proved to be the case. All things considered, Chavez thought it was the best that he could do.

His main job was to look out for the safety of his men and to direct them in suppression of the enemy. Within those general guidelines, lacking more specific orders from above, he had a fair amount of latitude. A victory would cover most mistakes that he might make. Conversely, if he failed...

Chavez didn't dwell on that prospect, either, for he knew that failure in the present circumstances would mean the end of his career, at the very least.

15

The rebel camp had started to calm down a bit when Bolan made it back. Sentries were posted, but the young men on the picket line were visibly distracted by the action taking place inside the compound, glancing backward frequently, less interested in standing watch than making sure they weren't left behind. The Executioner slipped past them easily—so easily, in fact, that he suspected it might be a trap.

But he was wrong.

The rebels were not laying bait for anybody. They were bailing out.

It was a clumsy process, with no vehicles, but the officers in charge were bawling orders at the rank and file, directing them as they collected weapons, loaded ammunition magazines to make the transport more efficient, broke down the communications gear and loaded it in several heavy-looking packs. A minipowwow near the communications tent told Bolan everything he had to know about the sudden agitation to evacuate: three soldiers staring at the slit cut in the tent and arguing among themselves.

So, they had found his handiwork and drawn the only logical conclusion. There was probably no way for them to tell whom he had spoken to, unless they knew the standard frequency for the security police in Lima, but the damage they had suffered, plus the threat of possible exposure to the world outside their hideaway, had prompted them to flee.

Where were they going? Bolan didn't give a damn. Chavez and company were coming *here*—assuming they showed up at all—and it would ruin everything if they arrived too late, to capture only burned-out huts and vehicles, a few stray tents and articles of military gear.

Whatever destination they might have in mind, the rebels were prepared to travel light. At one end of the camp, two soldiers were already dousing the collected corpses of their friends with gasoline, about to light them up and save the time required for digging graves. The wounded had been gathered in another section of the compound, under guard, and from the way the riflemen assigned to them were fidgeting, Bolan suspected they hadn't been chosen simply for protection.

It made perfect sense, of course. Guerrilla armies throughout history have lived or died according to mobility. If there was time to care for wounded soldiers, well and good; if not, when they became a liability, they were eliminated—for the greater good, of course. It was more merciful to shoot them outright than to place them in the hands of government interrogators, and less risky for the movement, too.

He understood the rationale and wasn't shaken by the prospect of those wounded soldiers being killed before his eyes. In fact the only reason they were still alive was that his own shots, or the shrapnel from his own grenades, had failed to strike a vital spot. It didn't matter in the least who pulled the trigger, just as long as it was done.

What troubled Bolan now was how he could prevent the rebels from escaping, keep them there until the cavalry arrived. And if the hoped-for reinforcements never came, if Chavez never got his message, or was otherwise unable to respond in time—what then?

Then he would have to tough it out alone, as he had done so many times before.

He reckoned that the main column, some sixty men in all, would leave the camp before the rear guard started executing wounded men. A short head start would ward off any risk of a potential mutiny and see most of the rebels on their way. It would be ten or fifteen minutes' work to kill the others, douse the stiffs with gasoline and light them up. If they were quick about it, the disposal team could catch up with their comrades in three-quarters of an hour, give or take.

It would be Bolan's task to stop the main guerrilla force from slipping out, and he would have to strike in such a way that his intended targets didn't flee in all directions, either, like a pack of frightened children.

Reaching for a 40 mm MECAR round, he moved up toward the firing line.

MAJOR PADILLA'S fighting column was within a quarter mile of the selected map coordinates when an explosion echoed through the forest. He couldn't pinpoint the distance or direction, more than to be sure that it was fairly close and somewhere up ahead of them.

Padilla's driver hit the brakes, thereby furnishing his commander with an opportunity to rise and summon his foot soldiers forward, urging some of them to fan out through the trees, while others formed a spearhead on the road and started double-timing forward. Padilla and his driver brought up the rear.

They started taking fire within a minute, ninety seconds at the most. It was sporadic, uncoordinated, automatic weapons rattling in the trees on both sides of the road. Padilla recognized the sound of AK-47s, with a shotgun blast thrown in from time to time, and he knew his own men carried M-16s. When they began to return fire, sometimes without a clear-cut target, the surrounding forest echoed like an army firing range.

The jeep was slowing, almost imperceptibly at first, Padilla's driver hunched behind the wheel, trying to make a smaller target of himself and so outwit the snipers in the forest.

"Hurry up!" Padilla snapped at him. "You drive like an old woman!"

Reluctantly the driver put more weight on the accelerator, and the jeep began to pick up speed. Padilla estimated that the site of the explosion had to be close now, possibly within a hundred meters or less. He clutched his submachine gun tightly, ready to unleash a stream of deadly fire if any target should present itself.

Padilla never knew exactly where the bullets came from, but he witnessed their effect up close and personal. One moment they were jolting over ruts and jutting stones; the next their windshield suddenly imploded, as if smitten by a giant fist. The driver's head snapped back, blood spattering Padilla in the shotgun seat, warm on his face. The jeep swerved to his right, a dead hand on the steering wheel. The trees were rushing at him when Padilla jumped to save himself.

He skinned his palms and bruised one shoulder and dropped his submachine gun in the scramble, but he retrieved it quickly, breaking for the nearest trees as soon as he could get his balance back. This time he heard the shots as snipers opened up on him, their bullets humming through the air like bumblebees. Padilla made it to the tree line and let the shadows cover him, moving forward, worried now that he might be cut off and isolated from his troops.

They had to be close if they were taking this much fire. It was too much for a coincidence. He should have been excited at the prospect of firm contact with the enemy, but he was shaken by his own close brush with death so early in the fight. It suddenly occurred to him that he and his men might be outnumbered by the enemy, in which case they would almost surely die, but arrogance had been part of Padilla's personality since childhood, and it didn't fail him now. He told himself that he was facing peasants, poorly trained, regardless of their numbers. They wouldn't prevail against a strike force of professionals.

As for himself, he could emerge the hero of the battle without taking any rash, extraordinary risks himself. The officer in charge was deemed responsible for any victory, regardless of his personal participation, and Padilla had already seen more action on this day than any other ranking officer of the security police would see within a given year. He smiled at that, the legend he was building for himself, and thought how handsome he would look when he put on a general's stars.

But first he had to make it through the afternoon alive.

Padilla almost stumbled on a body sprawled across his path. He checked the uniform and saw that it was one of his. There was no point in looking at the face, since he didn't know any of his men as individuals, couldn't have readily identified one if they passed each other on the street wearing civilian clothes. The corpse meant nothing to him, other than the fact that he had one man less to help him kill the enemy.

The major stepped across the corpse and kept on going. He heard more explosions and heavy firing from a point some sixty yards ahead of him, still hidden by the trees. He couldn't see the battleground as yet, but he could smell it: gun smoke and some other kind…could that be burning flesh? He caught a whiff of gasoline, the marzipan aroma of plastic explosives and the stench of sudden death.

At least, Padilla thought, he was headed in the right direction.

Clinging to the Smith & Wesson submachine gun like some kind of holy talisman, he jogged through the trees, pursuing sounds and smells, until he caught his first glimpse of the killing ground.

ALONZO AGUILLAR WAS nearly frantic, but he dared not let his soldiers glimpse the turmoil that he felt inside. His iron-clad image was the only thing that kept the troops from breaking and running for their lives. He couldn't afford to lose them now. If they couldn't effect an orderly withdrawal, each and every one of them would die.

The first explosion had been absolutely unexpected, ripping into what was left of the arsenal. The blast had claimed at least two men and started ammunition popping in the flames like deadly popcorn on an open fire, wild bullets flying every which way in the camp.

A couple of his soldiers claimed it was a rocket or propelled grenade, and pointed to a portion of the tree line where they swore that the projectile had originated. That, in turn, had started several others firing aimlessly into the woods, ignoring Aguillar's command that they cease fire and save their ammunition for a target they could see.

And then, before he could control the soldiers in the compound, he heard firing from the sentries staked out on the road, due south of camp. At first, he thought their firing was a reflex, triggered by the battle noise from camp, but then he heard another set of automatic weapons answer theirs, and knew the camp would soon be under siege.

He wondered for a moment whether they would have to face the army or security police, but it was fruitless speculation, and he quickly gave it up. Whichever force was sent against him, Aguillar knew soldiers of the Shining Path couldn't expect a show of mercy from their enemies. The standard policy was shoot-to-kill, except in urban areas where prisoners were sometimes taken to appease the media. At that, a bullet in the heart or brain was preferable to being captured by the state, subjected to interrogation, maybe locked up in a stinking prison cell for years on end.

Better to go down fighting like a man than to be caged and whipped into submission. Alonzo Aguillar had done some time when he was seventeen and vowed that he would never spend another day in jail, if it meant dying in the jungle, where the ants and worms would make a meal of him.

He shouted orders to his soldiers, trying to rally them. It was chaotic in the camp now, the survivors running here and there, a handful of them trying vainly to put out the fire that had consumed their stock of surplus ammunition, others firing blindly into the woods. Incoming fire still rippled through the camp, as well, but Aguillar couldn't pinpoint its source. He saw one of his soldiers fall, and then another, sprawling to the ground and lying still in death. He tried to guess the general direction of the fire that struck them down, but it was hopeless.

One by one he rallied twenty-odd guerrillas in the shadow of his old command post, nothing but a useless shack now, scarred by bullet holes and shrapnel marks. He tried to psych them up, infuse them with the fighting spirit that would be their only saving grace, if they should find the camp surrounded. All of them seemed ready for a fight, and Aguillar instructed them to fan out through the camp, find one or two more men each and bring them back immediately for instructions.

As they scattered, Aguillar stayed under cover, peeking out to see if he could spot the enemy, but they had obviously been engaged some distance down the narrow road that served the camp. He still had time to mount a passable defense, if only he could stop his soldiers from wasting bullets on the trees and forest shadows.

Once the rebel leader had his troops in place and battle had been joined, he could take steps to save himself. Assuming that the camp wasn't surrounded, he could take off through the woods and leave the others to delay his adversaries with a rearguard action, while he made a break to safety. Even knowing that the state had somehow found his secret base, there was no reason to believe they knew that he was there. One rebel, more or less, wouldn't be missed when it was time to make the body count. And if his soldiers were victorious—a circumstance that he didn't regard with optimism, at the moment—Aguillar could always fabricate some explanation for his own precipitate retreat. It was a military leader's obligation to preserve himself from harm, as long as he could better serve the cause in life than through a martyr's death.

BOLAN HEARD the steady firing from his right rear, the direction of the road, and wondered how Chavez could manage to attack from that direction, to the south, when Lima lay to the northwest. There had been insufficient time for any kind of motorized brigade to make the drive from Lima and push northward to the battle site. It could be done, of course, if they had come by air, but why, then, would they circle wide around the camp and come in on the southern side?

He was inevitably drawn to the conclusion that some other force had found the camp, either by luck or by having eavesdropped on his radio alert to Captain Chavez. Either way, the party crashers were encountering resistance, slogging through the final hundred yards or so with rebels fighting bitterly for every inch of ground.

It didn't matter, at the moment, where the troops had come from, who was leading them or what they had in mind. It was enough for Bolan that they had prevented an evacuation of the camp. Alone, he would have been hard-pressed to keep the sixty-odd guerrillas from escaping, even if they fled by twos and threes, but with a flying squad of uniforms to help him, nothing was impossible.

He caught himself at that, remembering that these troops didn't know him from Adam. They could easily mistake him for a member of the Shining Path, and would be prone to shooting first, perhaps omitting questions altogether, in their eagerness to score a victory. If he revealed himself to anyone other than Captain Chavez, he could expect a bullet for his trouble, nothing more.

Bolan knew the rules, and he could live with them. It was the kind of combat the Executioner understood, the kind he cut his teeth on as a green recruit, and he wasn't afraid to push his luck until it snapped.

He had run out of solid targets for his grenades, left with a field of tents and soldiers seeking cover where there was none to be found. He chose a pair of runners, more or less at random, leading them by several feet before he stroked the Steyr's trigger, sending half a dozen rounds downrange.

The leader stumbled, spinning in midair as bullets ripped into his torso, slamming him to earth. The second runner tried to leap across his fallen comrade, but the first man's outstretched fingers caught his ankle in a death grip, tripping him and dragging him down. Before he had a chance to struggle free and rise again, the Executioner had found his mark and fired another short burst to complete the double play. His human target shuddered, tumbled over on his back and moved no more.

At once a burst of automatic fire ripped through the leaves above his head, and Bolan fell back from the firing line to find himself another vantage point. The sounds of combat from the road were drawing closer by the moment, as the new arrivals made their push, displacing sentries one by one. It shouldn't be much longer, he surmised, before the uniforms broke through and reached the camp. Meanwhile the Executioner had work to do, and he could always find another point on the perimeter from which to lay down his harassing fire.

He didn't need to kill all the guerrillas by himself, as if he were alone. The new arrivals from the south would have to do their share, as well, now that the larger battle had been joined. Whatever inroads Bolan made from this point on were simply frosting on the cake.

It startled Bolan for a moment when he recognized one of the rebels on the far side of the camp. He double-checked, confirming the ID, and offered up a silent word of thanks to luck or fate. Alonzo Aguillar was ten years older than the mug shot in his mental file, perhaps fifteen, but there was no mistaking him. Even if Bolan hadn't recognized the face, his leadership of the assembled terrorists was evident when others ran to him across the killing ground, received instructions and went off to do as they were told.

From all appearances, he was constructing a defensive line across the south side of the camp to meet the column of advancing soldiers. Even those who had been guarding wounded prisoners were called into the firing line, their charges left to live or die, according to the whims of chance. When he had gathered and positioned every rebel who could walk and hold a weapon, Aguillar stood watching for a moment, giving final orders, waiting for his enemies to show themselves.

A moment later, as they came through the trees, Bolan saw men in uniforms of the security police. Gunfire broke out on both sides of the line, but there was something else, as well—the distant sound of helicopters, moving in from the northwest.

Aguillar had heard it and seemed to know that he would never have a better chance to save himself. With one last glance in the direction of his men, the rebel leader turned and ran due north, deserting them.

The Executioner saw where his duty lay and struck off in pursuit.

"SMOKE UP AHEAD."

The pilot's voice reminded Chavez of the sound an insect might produce if it increased in size a hundredfold and somehow learned to speak. His headset seethed with static, but the words were audible. Reluctantly he slipped free of his seat belt, moving so that he could peer out through the windscreen, leaning in between the pilot and his mate.

There *was* smoke rising from the forest, maybe two kilometers ahead of them. Treetops all looked the same to Chavez, from the air, but he could sense that they were getting close.

"Coordinates?" he asked the pilot.

"Getting there. When we reach the smoke, we should be right on top of them."

"We need to land as close as possible," Chavez reminded him.

"I'll do my best."

Chavez went back to warn his men that they had almost reached their target, while the copilot addressed the other helicopters. Everyone was ready, faces grim and weapons fully loaded, hands white-knuckled where they gripped the guns. If anyone was frightened, he refused to let it show.

They all knew landing was the hard part. If the trees prevented them from setting down inside the camp, they would be forced to march through jungle, possibly for several hundred yards, against an enemy who was forewarned of their arrival. On the other hand, a touchdown in the camp itself, while obviously better from the aspect of surprise, still left them vulnerable to defensive fire while they were in the air or scrambling from the helicopters with a minimum of cover to protect them.

Either way, they were about to get a taste of hell.

Chavez was curious about the smoke. There was too much of it to mark a cooking fire, which meant that there was trouble in the camp. He wondered if Belasko had been forced to move alone, or if Padilla's men had traveled overland to strike the camp. In either case, a fire meant trouble, which, in turn, meant that the rebels would be on alert, less easy to surprise.

It didn't matter.

Chavez hadn't come this far to simply turn around and fly back to Lima without ever laying eyes upon the enemy. It would be dangerous; he had accepted that, and it was known to all his men. They were the best that he could find in Lima, none of them corrupt or facing charges for abusing helpless prisoners, crack fighters who had proved themselves in other clashes with the Shining Path. He would have been more easy in his mind with twice as many troops behind him, but he would make do with what he had.

"One minute," the pilot warned.

Chavez sat down in his seat and cinched the safety belt tightly across his lap. It wouldn't matter if they took a rocket going in, but he didn't intend to be the first man on the ground by means of falling out.

The last bit of the ride was like a roller coaster, making Chavez thankful for his safety belt. The helicopter swung in one direction, then the other, finally dipping forward as it started losing altitude. The captain peered through the open bay on his left side and caught a glimpse of trees that seemed to shoot up at an oblique angle from the earth below. He clutched his rifle, swallowed hard to keep the remnants of his breakfast down and waited for the chopper to stabilize.

At touchdown Chavez leaped from the helicopter, beckoning his men to follow. They had landed roughly in the middle of a clearing hacked out of the forest, once concealed by camou netting that had evidently burned in places and torn free in others, possibly from damage by explosions, which was evident throughout the camp. The netting covered tents and grass now, like some great moth-eaten carpet, giving extra traction to their boots as they advanced to meet the enemy.

The Shining Path guerrillas were arrayed along the south end of the camp, most of them facing southward, even though they had to have heard the choppers coming down. It took a moment for Chavez to understand, and then he recognized the uniforms of troops attacking from the south, exchanging gunfire with the rebels. They were officers of the security police, and Chavez would have bet his pension that Major Padilla was the reason for their presence. And if the man himself was on the scene, it meant that Chavez was outranked, compelled to do whatever he was told by the most senior officer on-site.

He pushed that problem out of mind and waved his troopers forward, taking full advantage of the evident distraction of their enemies. He would confront Padilla later, if it came to that, and put the best face on it that he could.

MAJOR PADILLA REACHED the camp shortly behind his troops. His face was scratched and bloody from his brisk dash through the trees, his uniform in disarray. His cap was gone, lost somewhere in the woods or maybe when he bailed out of the jeep. He neither knew nor cared.

He had his submachine gun, and the pistol on his hip.

His men were in the camp, and they had met the enemy in open battle. It was all he needed, all he had to know.

It was impossible for him to count the rebels who were facing down his troops, but it appeared to be a roughly even match. The camp was in a shambles, dark smoke rising overhead at several points, although Padilla couldn't see exactly what had happened. He remembered the explosions they had heard before the rebel sentries opened fire, back in the woods, and knew that something else had happened here, before and independent of his own arrival on the scene.

There was no time to puzzle that one out, as bullets started whining overhead. Padilla ducked and kept on moving, finger on the trigger of his SMG. He had no targets yet; it would mean firing through his soldiers, toward the enemy, and he was happy for the moment to remain behind the lines. He grimaced every time one of his soldiers fell, but they kept surging forward, cutting down the enemy, regardless of the losses they sustained.

The helicopters took him by surprise. Padilla hadn't called for help, deliberately avoiding contact with his Lima office after intercepting the broadcast intended for Chavez. What troops were these, arriving airborne from the north?

He recognized the markings on the foremost helicopter: it belonged to the security police. A sour taste rose in his mouth, as he imagined Captain Chavez rushing in to steal the glory, trying to rob Padilla of his moment in the sun. Worse yet, if Chavez had been ordered to the scene by someone higher up, Padilla would be cornered, forced to fabricate an explanation for his presence in the area. Instead of winning praise, he might wind up in line for discipline, perhaps demotion, if he couldn't satisfy the general staff that he had good and proper reason to be where he was, without advising anyone in Lima of his destination.

Clearly he would have to ditch the weak war-games-gone-bad scenario that he had planned to use in the beginning. No one would believe that he had stumbled on a rebel campsite accidentally, while forces were en route from Lima to attack the selfsame target. It was farcical, but he was in the middle of a battle now and found it difficult to concentrate on polished lies.

There would be time enough for talking when the smoke cleared, and the general staff would be inclined to listen with a lenient ear to the commanding officer who claimed—and documented—a resounding victory against the Shining Path. If he could win the day before Chavez and company had time to make a major contribution, then Padilla could be off the hook in terms of blame.

The helicopters had begun to land, the lead ship already disgorging troops in uniform. Was Chavez in the vanguard? It would be a golden opportunity to rid himself of the seditious captain if he got a clear shot in the middle of the fight, but that was almost hoping for a miracle. Meanwhile Padilla had a battle to direct, and he was drawing closer to the action with each step he took.

"Press on!" he shouted to his men, uncertain whether anyone could hear him with the roar of automatic weapons and the sound of helicopter rotor blades. It made no difference. If he was questioned later, even if he took a polygraph, he would be truthful in describing how he drove his men to crush the rebel troops.

Off to Padilla's right, a blur of motion in the corner of his eye brought him around. He was amazed to see a rebel charging past the right flank of his troops, unseen by any of the nearest officers and breaking toward the trees. Toward where Padilla stood.

The major saw his chance to score another minor victory. He brought up the Smith & Wesson submachine gun, aimed at the runner as he cocked one arm, as if to lob a stone. The moving target seemed to have no weapon. Smiling, Padilla squeezed the trigger, laying down a screen of fire that tore into the traitor's chest and staggered him, blood spurting from his mortal wounds.

It was a testament to dying strength that the terrorist stayed upright long enough to hurl a small, dark object at the soldier who had killed him. When the man toppled forward, sprawling on his face, Padilla saw the object wobbling through the air, becoming larger, more distinct, until it struck the earth three feet in front of him.

A hand grenade.

Padilla screamed and turned to run, but there was no time left. The blast enveloped him in flames and lifted him, a blazing rag doll, tumbling back to earth among the trees.

THE HELICOPTERS LANDED well behind Mack Bolan as he plunged into the trees, pursuing Aguillar. He hesitated for a moment, listening as best he could, and picked up the diminishing sounds of a body in motion, crashing through the undergrowth, northbound. With his direction verified, he set off once again, knees pumping as he ran.

He had no fear that Aguillar would manage to outdistance him, but Bolan *was* concerned about the prospect of an ambush. Worse, there was a chance that he might miss his quarry in the forest if the runner went to ground or climbed a tree and waited for him to pass by. It would take days to search the forest thoroughly, with troops to help him. He could never hope to do it on his own.

But luck was with him, seemingly. His quarry didn't pause or seek a place to hide. If Aguillar was conscious of his own pursuit, then he had put his faith in speed, rather than stealth. Bolan hung on, measured his strides and paced himself, prepared to go the distance if it came to that.

They were a mile and counting from the compound, sounds of gunfire fading in the distance, when it came to Bolan that he could no longer hear his prey. He froze and listened, picked up nothing, felt the short hairs rising on his nape as he moved forward slowly step by step.

A burst of automatic fire ripped through the bushes well ahead of Bolan, slightly to his left. He pitched face-forward, flattening himself behind a fallen tree, as bullets chewed the scenery around him.

Close, but no cigar.

Alonzo Aguillar called out to him in Spanish. Bolan, knowing that the shooter had him spotted, answered back in English.

"Give it up! You're out of time!"

"American? Who are you, gringo?"

"I'm a bill collector," Bolan answered, creeping forward, inch by inch. "You're overdue."

"This is about the other gringo and his *niña*, yes?"

"You're not as stupid as I thought," Bolan said, freeing up a frag grenade.

"You must be CIA, I think."

"Think what you want. You're bought and paid for."

"Then, by all means, you must do your worst."

The AK-47 stuttered, raking Bolan's cover, flinging wood chips high and wide. Still hidden, Bolan used his ears to get a fair fix on the shooter's distance and direction. It wasn't precise, but then again, it wouldn't have to be.

"Are you still breathing, gringo?"

Bolan crawled another six feet forward, as silent as a snake. He wondered if the troops back at the camp could hear the gunfire from his own position. He couldn't hear them anymore, but that could simply mean the battle had been won by one side or the other. Either way, it stood to reason that the victors would come looking if they thought another fight was under way.

Which meant that he was running out of time. Again.

"I think you try to fool me, gringo. This is what you call the playing pussy, yes?"

The terrorist leader needed an English lesson, Bolan thought, but bit his tongue. He needed all his breath and energy for what came next, a leap from cover, one arm whipping overhead to lob the grenade before he dropped back out of sight behind the log. Aguillar unleashed another burst of automatic fire, but it was swallowed by the blast of the grenade.

Bolan vaulted to his feet and rushed the site of the explosion, ready with the AUG. He found his adversary down on one knee, leaning on his AK-47 like a crutch, blood streaming from a scalp wound and assorted other injuries.

Aguillar saw him coming and tried to raise his rifle, but he never had a chance. The stream of fire from Bolan's weapon whipped across his chest and abdomen, propelling him backward, boot heels kicking as he sprawled back on the turf. A final tremor, and the leader of the Shining Path lay still.

All done.

He listened once again, still heard no sounds from the direction of the camp, and took it as his signal to be on his way. He had a long trek back to reach his hidden vehicle, and with security police in the vicinity, he might be forced to wait for darkness before he could depart. From there, he had the rugged highway back to Lima still in front of him.

And somewhere on the way, he just might pass the hostages whom he had helped to liberate. Where were they at that moment? How much longer would it be before they got a message to the U.S. Embassy and found relief?

He had done all he could for now, but there would still be time when he got back to Lima for another look around. If there were problems left to solve, the Executioner would be available.

But he would keep his fingers crossed.

There had been blood enough, and he was tired. The doomsday clock was winding down.

Content to walk alone for now, beneath a cloudless sky, he turned back to the south and started pacing off his journey, one step at a time.

EPILOGUE

"We picked them up last night," Brognola said. His voice was small and distant on the line, a world away from Bolan in the Southern Hemisphere. "No major injuries, from what I understand."

"The lady has some difficulties coming up at Benning."

"That's a fact," Brognola replied. "I wouldn't be surprised if someone took a peek at motive when they got around to judging her, but rules are rules, you know the drill."

"She'll make a righteous soldier if they let her stay."

"I hear you, Striker, but I don't have any strings to pull on that side of the fence."

"I wasn't asking," Bolan said. "A simple observation."

"Right." The big fed's skepticism came out as a chuckle, soft and far away.

"So, what about the rest of it?"

"Officially the Shining Path is still alive and well. They've been around for damned near thirty years, you know. I'm not sure anyone down there would know exactly what to do tomorrow if they disappeared."

"And unofficially?"

"They got their asses kicked," Brognola said. "I take the head counts with a grain of salt, all things considered, but the leadership was obviously decimated. That means more time wasted, while the juniors squabble over who should run the show. The bottom line, I'd say you set them back a year at least.''

Bolan thought of Captain Chavez. "Was there any word about the officers who led the sweep?"

"Some honcho named Padilla bought the farm," Brognola told him. "They're giving him a hero's funeral next week. My word—and this is strictly off the record—is that he was more a strong-arm bully than a leader. Locals have been calling him 'the Butcher' for a while now, and they weren't all Shining Path."

"There was a captain named Chavez," Bolan said.

"He'll be Major Chavez by the time you talk to him again. Apparently he held the thing together after this Padilla took his dive. That makes him flavor of the month, at least until he stubs his toe or makes some enemies upstairs."

"I have a hunch he knows his way around."

"Whatever. You've got bookings on the next flight out, unless you need some time."

"I'll do my sleeping in the air," Bolan said.

"Good idea. And off the record, State says thanks for helping out their man. That's from the top."

"Received and noted. I wonder..."

"What?" Brognola asked.

"I'd like to grab some R&R when I get back."

"Something specific? I can make arrangements, or—"

"I thought I'd make a run past Benning."

"Just for old times' sake?"

"Or something."

"Right. Well, I don't see a problem there. You'll keep in touch?"

"Sounds fair."

"So, I'll be talking to you."

"Affirmative."

"Stay frosty, guy."

"I wouldn't have it any other way."

He cradled the receiver, cutting off Brognola's laughter, and began the walk back to his car.

Under Attack!

STONY MAN™ 34

REPRISAL

In a brilliant conspiracy to restore the glory days of the CIA, a rogue agent has masterminded a plot to take out Company competition. His stolen clipper chip has effectively shut down the Farm's communications network and made sitting ducks of the field teams. With Phoenix Force ambushed and trapped in the Colombian jungle, and a cartel wet team moving in on Able Team stateside, it's up to Mack Bolan and the Stony experts to bring off the impossible.

Available in April 1998 at your favorite retail outlet.

Take
4 explosive books
plus a
mystery bonus
FREE

After the ashes of the great Reckoning, the warrior survivalists live by one primal instinct

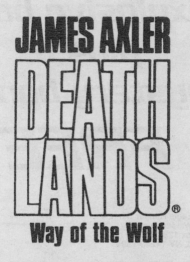

JAMES AXLER
DEATH LANDS®
Way of the Wolf

Unexpectedly dropped into a bleak Arctic landscape by a mat-trans jump, Ryan Cawdor and his companions find themselves the new bounty in a struggle for dominance between a group of Neanderthals and descendants of a military garrison stranded generations ago.